The CYCLE of CYRNOS

INK START MEDIA
5710 W Gate City Blvd Ste K #284
Greensboro, NC 27407

The CYCLE of CYRNOS

Book Three: The Pisan Interlude

By Pascal Paul Piazza

INTRODUCTION

This book completes the initial trilogy of the Cycle of Cyrnos. The first book explored the origins of the Corsican people from the Mesolithic to the Bronze Age, The second book developed the foundation of the Corsican people from the Bronze Age to the Preaching of the First Crusade and Pisa's acquisition of Corsica.

This third book reveals the transition that was the Pisan Peace in Corsica from 1092 to 1299. Pisa guided the development of Corsica rather than ruled Corsica. It built roads and churches. It enriched trade to and from Corsica. It helped to cultivate the genius of Corsica's freedom. It did so even though Genoa pressured Pisa this entire time by finding colonies, raiding, hindering trade and motivating the Corsican counts to fight Pisa and the Commune.

Pisa's interlude coincided with the Crusades. The Crusades occurred principally between 1095 (when Pope Urban II preached the First Crusade) to 1291 (the fall of Acre and the last Western outpost in the Holy Land or Outremer). The Crusades are ahistorical. The Crusades provide a medium to discuss the tensions between the idealism of the Crusades and the contradictions in behavior. Those tensions challenged the Corsican character which had to reconcile them. The Crusades did involve Corsica, although most histories ignore that involvement or give it passing mention. Corsica, situated as it was, on the main routes for, at a minimum, the first three Crusades had to play a major role. Corsica had to have robust ports and traders, available material for ships and siege materials, and an irresistible place to travel to (as it still is). Corsica also had to have its academies and scholars that helped shaped the minds of those that participated in the Crusades. The third book continues the plot line of the first two books that Corsica has had a larger role in history than most histories credit.

Pisa's interlude was populated with some of Corsica's most interesting persons whose stories will be highlighted. Corsican tradition has different versions of the stories of these colorful characters. Their stories told are an imaginary amalgamation of many of these stories. The third book ends with the exploits of Ghjudice della Rocca. His story is the Pisan Peace in summary. His story is the story of the heroes that will dominate Corsican history for the next six hundred years. His story reveals that Genoa may have been ceded Corsica, but Corsica's drive for freedom had just started.

These three books comprise an epic poem. I hope the reader enjoys them as much as I did to write them.

TABLE OF CONTENTS

BOOK EIGHTEEN

Pascal Paul Piazza
The Medieval Quintet: Corsica and the First Crusade
(From the taking of the Cross Up to the Coronation of King Baldwin I of Jerusalem)
– January 1096-December 25, 1100 CE

TASH

"The maquis is both marvel and mental.

It is a restive refuge and temple.

It ignites the fervent fire to be free.

It measures much more than the mind can see."

PATTI

"Fortitude is the true strength of the will.

Found in old ports and terraces to till.

No boundaries limit the force it employs.

It tracks true as the boar's baton deploys."

BERNADETTE

"Corsica was part of the journey east.

Pilgrims with arms seeking Heaven's soul feast.

Freeing the land and sins by the Tomb's might.

Restoring the Light of day overnight."

MARY

"The call was made to those who had no fears.

The first to join had fought the Moors for years.

Next came men no longer fighting the counts.

Then those to fulfill vendetta accounts."

CHARLOTTE

"Our vanguard went under Pisa's banners.

A complement to commercial Papal planners.

Hidden from history in their own right.

Their acts and courage kept them in plain sight."

Vincente of Propriano and Andrea of Pisa Captain Ships to Intercept the Moorish Capture of Pilgrims on Their Way to Filatosa – August 1096 CE

ANDREA

"It takes time to find a slave ship on the run,

Stealth Saracen sails hide under the sun.

Our two ships must rescue the pilgrims lost.

We have but one goal regardless of cost."

VINCENTE

"Fifty years do not mitigate the pain.

Thoughts of these slaves for sale drive me insane.

Let fire remind them of the Moor's birth-place.

Devils on earth from an ungodly race."

ANDREA

"Birds fear the shrill call piercing our ears.

The slave chant signals us to hear their fears.

We can now find the Moor ship leaving no trace.

And bestow upon it some redeeming grace."

VINCENTE

"They fight with such skill as a fervent foe.

They will die adrift by a death so slow.

Our goal is done and no slaves will be sold.

We gave them a gift much greater than gold."

ANDREA

"Hand-to-hand we fought on this joyful day.

They float dead or half-alive who can say?

Prayers abound as the dominant sound.

Some to die soon and others to find ground."

VINCENTE

"There is one who made land before dusk's light.

He seems solemn and not ready to fight.

Does he rest before he leaves on his way?

What he intends is quite hard to say!"

RODRIGO

"You and I arrive on this hidden shore.

You are home while I am a guileless Moor.

You can kill me now to complete your day.

But, let me sit here and enjoy the spray."

VINCENTE

"I will wait, but you give me no real choice.

Your caprice takes our children while you rejoice.

You will not trade with us or sell us goods.

You just want to build more ships from our woods."

RODRIGO

"My choice die, convert or pay a tax.

New strict Moors rule as others were too lax.

I chose the tax and was told to come here.

The wars with the north are costly I fear."

VINCENTE

"Pisa builds the coast and adds to its fleet.

To prepare its defense in both cold and heat.

Tell your new masters to stay far away.

I too will sleep soundly in the cool spray."

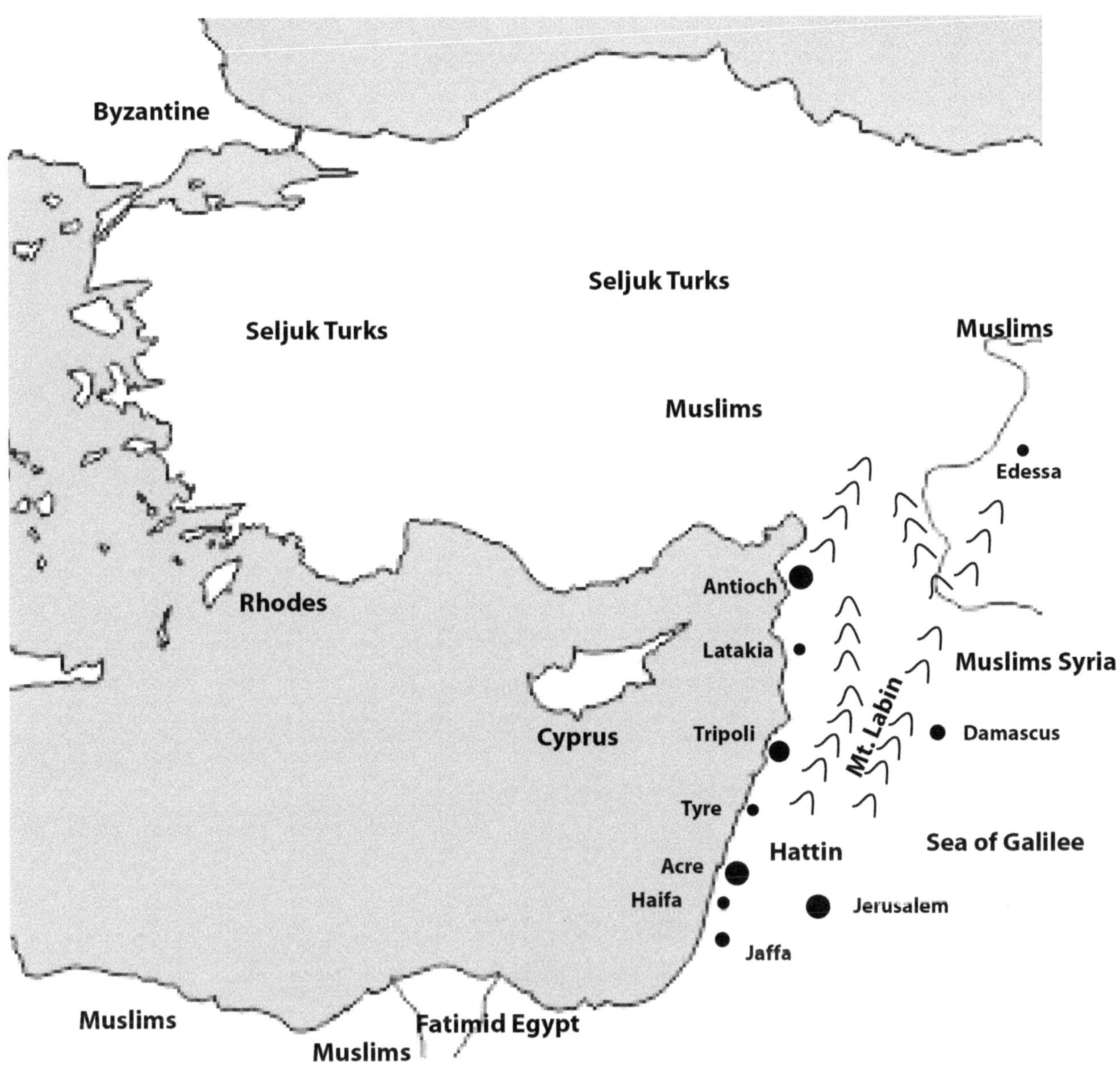

The Holy Land During the Preaching of the First Crusade —1095 CE

Pascal Paul Piazza

Ghjustu and Onestu Look for Vincente on the Journey South to Find Soldiers to Take the Cross – August 1096 CE

VINCENTE

"During my sleep I have stopped to bleed.

I am alone keeping secret my creed.

Wait, who comes with a pace pensive but slow?

What is your commune and who do you know?"

GHJUSTU

"Brandu by birth, but I seek a new home.

I know our true Lord who asks us to roam.

God wills it we fight the Muslims and win.

At His Tomb we get remission of sin."

VINCENTE

"Are you Corsican or some Pisan breed?

Should not my sins be gone with my last deed?

We have fought the Moors for three hundred years.

Yet, all we received was blood, sweat and tears."

ONESTU

"We felt the same way when we heard the call.

We thought it sinister simony's pall.

But, we are to liberate His lost land.

We will be pilgrims at the Tomb so grand."

VINCENTE

"We always must be true, steadfast and fair.

Freedom is our soul and our pure prayer.

With these traits, let us all wear the one cross.

Anything other than these traits is pure gloss."

ANDREA

"Our ships soon sail to the Provençal port.
We bring more goods for the Occitan court.
You three can join Raymond's growing host.
He will travel East inland from the coast."

ONESTU

"So Pisa reaps gold from our longtime trade.
Its ships following the course we have made.
Narbo and Toulouse are well known to us.
Two thousand years lay open with no fuss."

GJUSTU

"We abhor counts regardless of his name.
We will not journey East to build his fame.
We are pilgrims and not serfs at his call.
We serve just our Lord and no count at all."

VINCENTE

"We have counts who offer money to fight.
We will decline when they are out of sight.
We still march with them just to keep us well.
When the Moors attack you never can tell."

ANDREA

"Then serve the chaplain Raymond as he quests.
Do you think he authors one of the gestes?
Three pilgrims will not survive the trip East.
A larger host is needed at the least."

Jacopo the Pisan and Fieru of Aleria Travel
From Ghisoni to the Valley of Niolo Via Vizzavona – December 1098 CE

JACOPO

"This path appears from nowhere in cut stone.

The rut hides cool flows that will chill the bone.

Green swaths entice the goat as my guide.

Ah, rocks break my fall while you mock my pride."

FIERU

"Never follow a goat on its pure path.

It goes up and down which leads us to wrath.

The devil cut rough stone to make us bleed.

Her Grace smoothed the way so we are freed."

JACAPO

"We build wharves and ports to restore trade.

Each new wide road receives a Roman grade.

We gather men to free the lost Holy Land.

Yet, I seek to lead, but still cannot stand."

FIERU

"You must join the land and not try to win.

The conquest of the stone is our great sin.

Taking the Cross still leaves our normal life.

Whom we leave here will suffer joy and strife."

JACAPO

"The Commune and counts ready men to fight.

That is a wrong that a Truce must make right.

Niolo's valley must feel a new peace.

Our ships must go East to find the lost fleece."

Stella and Fidelia, Daughters of Niolo, Converge on the Spring of Niolo at the Same Time as the Counts Cinarca and Ganelon

FIDELIA

"Two armies approach our land for battle.

Counts want more estates and much more chattel.

The Commune fosters freedom not a king.

None of that impacts us or our pure spring."

STELLA

"Father and other shepherds may not fight.

But that does not make their decision right.

I keep their word and keep prey from the herd.

I wash fox blood from my thigh with no word."

COUNT CINARCA

"Let my firm hand help you wash the blood clean.

Such gifts as you two have never been seen.

You should well welcome my hand and my eye.

This count's gaze will raise your status so high."

STELLA

"I will gut you just like the fox today.

No man will try to touch me in that way.

There is water to cleanse your blood from me.

A pike will hold your head for all to see."

COUNT GANELON

"My friend jokes, as he is a tired bore.

He will retreat as does the beaten boar.

We mean no dishonor and seek your grace.

We will not forget though your leg and face."

Pascal Paul Piazza

Niolo Entertains the Podesta Leader of the Commune's Troops on the Banks of the Lac de Nino

NIOLO

"What is your village and why are you here?
We are but shepherds you should never fear.
You would not want to know where we are now.
We are still free and we will never bow."

PODESTA

"We are from Nebbiu seeking your aid.
Our army does not fear the peace you made.
War is near and blood soon covers the bogs.
We need more mobile men, weapons and dogs."

NIOLO

"Our dogs are needed to control the herds.
I care about my own and not your words.
This does not involve my clients or friends.
Joining the war will yield grief with no ends."

PODESTA

"Our Commune fights to keep all of us free.
The counts, unlike us, will not let you be.
They will find you and then not let you hide.
Your freedom mandates that you join our side."

NIOLO

"The land is the only mandate we need.
The Moors do not care much where our herds feed.
Pisa builds roads and ports but nothing here.
His Tomb remains free to goats, sheep and deer."

Niolo is Upbraided by His La Donna Signadore

LA DONNA SIGNADORE

"Why do rebuke men trying to help you?

You know the name of each spring, pass and ewe.

But, you ignore your duty that you owe.

You are not an eagle but just a crow."

NIOLO

"I protect all we care for from the fight.

How can you say what I do is not right?

If we come down now our herds will be lost.

Our freedom will follow as our true cost."

LA DONNA SIGNADORE

"Your honor is lost if you stay and hide.

Lust for your daughter now fuels a count's pride.

Yet, no father will defend his true trust.

He does not act now and do what he must."

NIOLO

"Your words are clever, but they make no sense.

They do not move me; they just make me tense.

There has been no attack as you suggest.

There is no defilement to start a quest."

LA DONNA SIGNADORE

"A count tried to feel Stella's thigh last night.

She sought revenge with such passion and might.

The counts then left fast before she could strike.

She sought to impale their heads on her pike."

Niolo Joins the Order of Battle of the Army of the Commune

PODESTA

"How is it the birds know we will soon fight.

They cackle laughing at us in their flight.

Our few troops flock too to protect the lake.

Loose lines now draw tightly for freedom's sake."

CARLO

"The counts will charge with horse, ax, mail and mace.

We will stand tall together face to face.

We must force their ranks to fight in the bogs.

If they gain the flanks, we will fall like logs."

NIOLO

"The battle is won before it is fought.

We set the trap before the prey is caught.

They seek to surround you by mountain path.

But an ambush will close each path with wrath."

PODESTA

"Then they must meet us on the soggy plain.

Our hope to win welcomes the restive rain.

Thank God the shepherds have come to our aid.

But, why did you change the choice you had made?"

NIOLO

"Do you care why if we now join your host?

The counts lack honor and just like to boast.

My daughters seek vengeance at all cost.

Freedom is pure and can never be lost."

The Counts Deploy – The Counts' Order of Battle

COUNT GANELON

"What do we seek from another battle?

We cannot take some land or steal chattel.

Our spies tell us Pisans march here this day.

Their mobile troops will command this sharp fray."

COUNT CINARCA

"My friend, your fear of a fight fills old tales.

Yet, we do not fight to claim land or wells.

We show power the free man has to fear.

The long struggle will end within the year."

Captain of the Horse

"The coarse horse mail glistens in the bright sun.

They have no horse so this battle is won.

We fill the passes to surround their host.

The chestnuts and boar here make a great roast."

COUNT GANELON

"Wait, we now have word from our flanking men.

They have been caught like spring pigs in a pen.

The horse then must cover the soggy ground.

Where they will bog down stuck in a muck mound."

COUNT CINARCA

"We shall compel a win without any fight.

We should parley now long before the night.

Do we care if some old men have been lost.

We question if they can suffer the cost?"

Counts Cinarca and Ganelon Meet Niolo and a Podesta before the Battle

NIOLO

"We will meet, but we will not discuss terms.

Soon your cool blood will cover the lake berms.

Your flanking troops are dead where they are found.

Horse cannot move over the futile ground."

COUNT CINARCA

"Your daughters now roam alone in these hills.

My lust sends me out for more of my thrills.

We will hunt them down as the prey they are.

Your vengeance will not get then very far."

NIOLO

"A flag of truce protects your lurid tongue.

See the hook on which your heart will be hung.

But my feelings do not guide us this day.

Your feckless force will fast foreclose this fray."

PODESTA

"There can be no plan to deploy your horse.

We fear nothing to behead your full force.

We so abhor that so much blood will flow.

But, we will do so as the wind does blow."

COUNT GANELON

"Pisa will not let such carnage occur.

The Pope will soon banish you and your cur.

Their bold banners can be seen in plain sight.

We can all foresee who wins today's fight."

JACAPO

"The banners of Pisa arrive this day.

They ripple in the wind with words to say.

The flags of the counts are lost in our might.

Our pike and phalanx control all in sight."

BISHOP OF MARIANA

"I declare the Truce of God for all here.

Disobey and it is God you will fear.

Each vendetta ends now with no more blood.

As one, we ravage the East like a flood."

COUNT CINARCA

"We do not recognize Pisa's clerics.

You lack the mantle of any true relics.

We have the better order on this field

I order you to make the Commune yield."

FIERU

"You will bog down and then quickly retreat.

God though wants neither side to feel defeat.

We must rally now as Antioch falls.

We must meet now around His City's walls."

THE BISHOP OF MARIANA

"Bishop Daimbert leaves with Pisa's fleet.

We bring siege engines, supplies, wax and wheat.

He is the Pope's Legate bringing order.

The Sea welcomes him without a border."

NIOLO

"We have no fight in the East as we speak.

My village keeps me strong and never weak.

Revenge lies open here and fuels my soul.

I need not kill Muslims to become whole."

STELLA

"Why do we not begin this needed fight.

If we wait longer, it will become night.

This knife must turn that ram into an ewe.

My honor demands what I am now due."

FIERU

"Sheathe your stringent sword, soul and spirit too.

Save it for the Saracens you will slew.

Who joins us to make the Holy Land free?

To reap vengeance on the Muslims we see?"

FIDELIA

"If she goes to war, it is not alone.

She lacks the bad deeds for her to atone.

I will be by her side through thick and thin.

We together will force our troops to win."

BISHOP OF MARIANA

"We leave from Aleria within the week.

I now will help you find that what you seek.

These Corsicans will now march off to war.

Bearing the beloved baton of the boar."

The Pisan Armada Invests Latakia – September 1099 CE

STELLA

"One hundred and twenty ships are power.

They can lift spirits or make one cower.

But we attack islands with Christ's minions.

Freeing goods and not Moorish dominions."

FIERU

"But, now we arrive in the Holy Land.

The ships array for a campaign so grand.

We surely blockade some major home port.

To curtail the spread of some Moorish tort."

FIDELIA

"Are we pilgrims here watching some old dock?

We crowd tight in pens like a feckless flock.

Ten ships each contain thirty of our race.

The baton is silent leaving no trace."

JACAPO

"Bohemond leads this battle at this time.

He best knows when the time to siege is prime.

Antioch and His City fell to him.

These Byzantines must now release their whim."

STELLA

"The stories of their deeds are not complete.

We will not know the extent of their feat.

But, I will not blindly follow any count.

While bodies of Christians start to mount."

FIERU

"Your words remain true after one long week.

This is not the goal we left home to seek.

Yet wait they signal us now to make land.

You may not have to kill him by your hand."

FIDELIA

"Let us give thanks for a safe trip on the sea.

I will form the three hundred around me.

I hold the baton high in my right hand.

The mighty boar readies to free this land."

VINCENTE

"Three years ago, I last saw my home land.

I arise to praise that baton so grand.

I have felt hunger's pangs and desert thirst.

And the sweetest wins absolving the worst."

ONESTU

"The counts justly control what has been won.

But sacrifice paid is quickly undone.

This siege hurt an ally that we all need.

We must not draw blood over the same creed."

GHJUSTU

"Adhemar the Legate kept the counts true.

The clerics helped us know what to do.

We escort the new Legate and you too.

We still remain forthright, loyal and true."

The Journey from Latakia to Jerusalem

STELLA

"The land is wide, but the path is narrow.

It is a cut course that chills the marrow.

We cannot move to the left or the right.

We pass among island towns in our sight."

FIERU

"Some Muslims greet us with gifts and money.

Should we fear those bringing wax and honey?

Cold eyes survey from the stone with disdain.

Will arrows soon fall like a hot rain?"

FIDELIA

"Why did we not stop at that Christian town?

It seems the world has turned upside down.

How can we know true friend from infidel?

Are we at home in a Moor's citadel?"

VINCENTE

"Your eyes witness strands of a curious tale.

One prince wears silk while the other wears mail.

They pray with one hand and rule with a fist.

They succor the poor while truth is a cyst."

ONESTU

"I saw counts walk barefoot with humble airs.

And ration death with no certain cares.

Some princes free captives spilling no blood.

Others fill the streets with a sanguine flood."

GHJUSTU

"The emirs are the same and share the lust.
Counts and sultans are whirlwinds of the dust.
It is the same in Lorraine or in Homs.
They are warriors with estates as home."

JACAPO

"We are where Christ first set foot on the land.
Where He died saving us all with His hand.
That is why the Holy Lance saved the siege.
And why parts of His Cross led his true liege."

VINCENTE

"We walk well among the first Christian tribes.
Are they heretics like the temple scribes?
Some welcome us while others want us dead.
That is why some towns signal certain dread."

ONESTU

"Muslims pay us fees as they favor work.
They want our rich trade and they hate the Turk.
They too believe saints brought us many wins.
Yet, we lose when we again commit sins."

GHJUSTU

"This is a world where counts and kings fight.
Clerics lack power to dispel the night.
You know what it is that you truly see.
We are not serfs, but forthright and free."

JACAPO

"This king in Jerusalem seeks our aid.

Three hundred fresh new troops will well be paid.

He extends power far beyond his walls.

But, the Moors lie in wait as the night falls."

FIERU

"We do not care who rules Antioch's fee.

We have come to make the Holy Land free.

The Bishop may make Bohemond his friend.

But, the purpose of our quest does not end."

STELLA

"We said we would escort the Legate south.

Yet, I do want to hear words from his mouth.

That he comes to bring order to the counts.

That this host of good friends make good accounts."

VINCENTE

"We will fight well as we always have done.

Pisa's banner will herald battles won.

We won for Rome, the Visi and the Franks.

We did do, as now, with no need for thanks."

FIDELIA

"We will present the Legate as we must.

But we are free; bound by our sacred trust.

The land across the Sea changes us not.

Our true soul cuts through the Gordian knot."

Meeting Between Godfrey of Lorraine, Advocate of Jerusalem, and Daimbert, Papal Legate, in Jerusalem – Christmas 1099 CE

DAIMBERT

"Your complete wins must have been Heaven sent.

We will never know the blood and pain spent.

Five counts and no king invites disorder.

Yet, the Holy Land is free in good order."

GODFREY

"That freedom succeeds is a fragile fact.

We need men and ships without a cleric's tact.

Pisa's many ships can secure the coast.

Baldwin and Normans can meet Duqaq's boast."

DAIMBERT

"You all must know that there should not be kings.

The Pope rules this Land without counts with rings.

Many fervent souls died because the princes fought.

A cleric's tact brought you the wins you sought."

GODFREY

"Arnulf is weak with little good to say.

His patron, Robert, returns home this day.

I need more Norman knights and Lorraine's best.

Pisa's ships can supply all of the rest."

BOHEMOND

"Baldwin and I will sortie this next morn.

Pisan ships will supply weapons and corn.

We seal our support in this robust way.

Daimbert too should be Patriarch this day."

Daimbert, now Patriarch of Jerusalem, Returns to Meet with Godfrey, Advocate of Jerusalem, in Jerusalem – February 1100 CE

DAIMBERT

"Raymond and you choose not to be a king.

Yet, you want the power our help will bring.

We gave you the strength to extend your reach.

Emirs plead as your foes fall in the breach."

GODFREY

"You are a pawn if blind to Norman guile.

You succumb to your new trappings and style.

Antioch laughs if you and I still fight.

We are well beyond Bohemond's short sight."

DAIMBERT

"Bohemond invites me to meet the Pope's plan.

Baldwin ignores me as best as he can.

Tancred rules Galilee as his own state.

Raymond still sulks around Tripoli's gate."

GODFREY

"Do you know what is it that you now ask?

You impose on me too great of a task.

My men died and paid the ultimate cost.

How do I say what we won now is lost?"

DAIMBERT

"You were true pilgrims on a freedom quest.

Valor and death show your men were the best.

Jaffa and the City must pass in your will.

This is not the place for time to stand still."

Daimbert, Patriarch of Jerusalem, Joins the Attack on Acre – July 1100 CE

JACAPO

"Godfrey is sick and gasps from his death bed.

He is weak having had the last rites read.

Yet, he resists the transfer as he must.

Venice and Lorraine fuels this breach of trust."

VINCENTE

"These thieves will invest Acre this fortnight.

We must show them who controls this new fight.

The boar will lead our troops into the war.

Being faithful to the oath that they swore."

STELLA

"We owe no fealty to the Bishop's pride.

We should all be present at Godfrey's side.

To make sure that that City remains free.

That is what the oath I takes means to me."

FIDELIA

"The clergy still plays its role in the East.

They curtail counts who countenance the Beast.

The Holy Cross or Lance led the true way.

But, now they are lost and they hold no sway."

FIERU

"Our women alone speak what is so right.

We ill serve our God fighting just for spite.

Yet, we must honor our Pisan compact.

Even if our blood boils making us react."

Godfrey Dies as Tancred and Daimbert Redeploy Their Forces from Acre to Haifa – July 1100 CE

TANCRED

"We waste our finest troops at Acre's gate.

Godfrey's dead and we cannot act too late.

Shift the war to Haifa to show power.

While I also move on David's Tower."

DAIMBERT

"Are you certain that this is the right plan?

Let us wait for Bohemond if we can.

I wrote a letter asking him to rule.

I made it look just like a Bishop's bull."

TANCRED

"I did not think you would hesitate.

Our actions govern not the whim of fate.

New orders have already been given.

My rashness is a sin to be forgiven."

DAIMBERT

"I will stay with the troops at the new siege.

I will ensure that you are Haifa's liege.

Godfrey may cede this town to another.

But, you have many more troops for cover."

JACAPO

"The Corsicans scaled the walls today.

Haifa fell quickly without much delay.

Tancred's banners fly to make a statement.

Women parade in their finest raiment."

The Struggle for the Kingdom of Jerusalem and the Coronation of King Baldwin I – September-December 1100 CE

DAIMBERT

"Godfrey's will left this City just to me.

Yet, Warner will not let this devise be.

Words will not cede power to the true Church.

We waste time as we still stand in the lurch."

TANCRED

"Warner's guards strongly hold David's Tower.

But, they do not hold the keys to power.

Warner has sent for Baldwin to march here.

We cannot lose pace as Baldwin draws near."

DAIMBERT

"Fear not, as I have foreseen such a ploy.

Soon such sadness will replace Warner's joy.

I ask Bohemond to stop Baldwin fast.

Baldwin's relief will be lost in the past."

JACAPO

"I bring bad news to my Bishop this day.

No help from Antioch is on its way.

Raymond read your letter with great dismay.

Your true servant has now been held at bay."

TANCRED

"I receive word that Baldwin nears Haifa's gate.

I march there now in force to find our fate.

His men and mine have fought for blood before.

It is time that I even the past score."

BALDWIN

"Haifa and Jaffa fell in due order.

Tancred has left for Galilee's border.

Daimbert seeks refuge in Mount Sion's halls.

Soon the rest of this kingdom surely falls."

ARNULF

"Warner is dead, but Godfrey's guards remain.

Neither Church nor Norman foreclose your reign.

Godfrey was just too easily misled.

Punish him who got a will from his bed."

BALDWIN

"I gladly assume the title of king.

Let me review the gifts my subjects bring.

Tancred returns Galilee to my house.

Bring me Daimbert to bow low like a mouse."

DAIMBERT

"I pray for the new king from my monk's cell.

Your rise to such fame is a tale to tell.

Godfrey did not take the crown as he could.

Accept the gold crown from me if you would."

BALDWIN

"You are still Patriarch with Rome's power.

I will not jail you in a cold tower.

Bowing to me is the price you will pay.

You will crown me true king on Christmas Day."

STELLA

"We came as pilgrims to free this lost land.

On our true oath and not a mission grand.

The counts who agree now travel back West.

The others rule by the cross on their vest."

FIERU

"Godfrey was protector and not a king.

Raymond also chose to reject the ring.

Baldwin though put all that charade aside.

He employs royal fiat with great pride."

FIDELIA

"Counts may treat each city like their own pawn.

Fighting Moors at dusk while allied at dawn.

We must act to help the lordless stay free.

Our path now leads beyond Tiberius' Sea."

VINCENTE

"Pisa remains for the trade we can make.

Christians, Moors and Turks have markets to take.

The counts reject oaths to the Pope or kings.

They grant the charters that free commerce brings."

WICKHAM

"Stella's critique of the counts is correct.

Feudal rule fills the void without respect.

Outremer, France and her isle suffer the same.

Communes resist with freedom's fulsome flame."

BOOK NINETEEN

Pascal Paul Piazza

The Medieval Quintet: From the End of the First Crusade to the End of Balearic Crusade – 1100-1115 CE

TASH

"Corsicans saw the four-year journey end.

Was it all worth the price they had to spend?

Outremer was the die that freedom cast.

With too many counts, could liberty last?"

PATTI

"Stella was vacant having to serve kings.

She sought refuge among valleys and springs.

The diaspora brought life to her heart.

Mountains supply a new pure place to start."

BERNADETTE

"A return home was not a salve at all.

The boar then went West to answer the call.

The Cross may change the direction it takes.

There are so many relics that are fakes."

MARY

"The Moors still sail to find slaves as they might.

One slave though built the arc of a long fight.

The battle began first on Spain's northwest coast.

And ends with a sheik's death and village boast."

CHARLOTTE

"For three-hundred years Pisa did rule well.

The Levant trade saw many goods to sell.

Pisa though had to fight envy's green eyes.

Surrounded by merchants, savants and spies."

The Cycle of Cyrnos
**Crossroads Stella, Fidelia, Fieru and the Corsican Host Leave Jerusalem
for Three Villages in Mount
Liban Through Galilee and Past the Horns of Hattin – 1105 CE**

FIERU

"Daimbert and Bohemond soon leave for Rome.

It is time we all return to our home.

We were pilgrims doing that what we swore.

We met our oath of the cross that we wore."

STELLA

"Daimbert was in exile at Baldwin's hand.

Twice he quickly had to leave this land.

He was but a pure pawn in Tancred's game.

To restore him twice just built Tancred's fame."

FIDELIA

"Once Daimbert could not say the Easter Mass.

Until bribes for Baldwin made a sure pass.

Then Daimbert kept his own vast horde of gold.

So he lost his seat to a monk's cell cold."

JACAPO

"Daimbert seeks the Pope's sure ear to plead.

He goes with Bohemond who now will lead.

The Norman host provides the force to see.

You have met your oath and now you are free."

FIERU

"We are far from home, yet we are at home.

The maquis follows us to where we roam.

Three small towns invite us to be in charge.

It is a commune that is not so large."

STELLA

"Yet, it is as if Niolo moved here.

We seek a refuge in stone without fear.

We pray that Mount Liban will be like home.

And we no longer later have to roam."

FIDELIA

"But, danger will track the road that we take.

The heat will make us burn, blister and bake.

Raids wait for us all on stone and on land.

Baldwin will not be there to lift a hand."

FIERU

"We are mobile strangers in a strange land.

This bold boar overwhelms stone, sea and sand.

We cannot ask why things may not be so.

There are larger questions we need to know."

STELLA

"Why do they ask us to come as they do?

Are we to stay or leave when we are through?

Do they know we bring no count, prince or king?

And that we will reject each crown and ring?"

FIDELIA

"Do they expect to see banners and flags?

Or pilgrims in bare feet and wearing rags?

Do they need to hear a sweat angel sing?

Will they want more than the freedom we bring?"

FIERU

"Look Hattin's Horns are a sure sight to see.

Soon we pass the shore of Galilee's Sea.

There is brush on the hills along the way.

It is dry kindling that could burn this day."

STELLA

"What is the smoke cloud that forms all around.

We soon cannot see the path on the ground.

The heat is intense and our throats are dry.

The horses will bolt if we let them try."

FIDELIA

"Muslims have set the kindling brush on fire.

They have set up a big blockade pyre.

Let us break to the left over the hill.

They will not know the deft depth of our skill."

FIERU

"Spray water on your horse and yourself too.

It is a small but important thing to do.

Your horse will not care that the flames are there.

They will charge with no real burden to bear."

MICHAEL

"Wait, as the fire will soon be put out.

We are here to protect your forthright route.

The Turks are dead or have run from the field.

We are your hosts, your buckler and shield."

GREGORY

"It is still a half-day ride in the heat.

There still may be traps set we have to beat.

You must have questions you wish to ask.

You will have time to consider your task."

YUSUF

"We mirror the tribes and land all around.

Abraham's kin all sharing the same ground.

Three enclaves of Christian, Arab and Jew.

Making one commune with a mountain view."

MICHAEL

"Maronites and Kurds tend to their large flocks.

Arabs and Jews conduct trade among the rocks.

Each tribe thinks and worships with their own rite.

We are all outcasts in Antioch's sight."

GREGORY

"Emirs, sheiks, princes and counts are the same.

We are a pawn in very deadly game.

We move back and forth just to build their fame.

It is the same if they are bold or tame."

YUSUF

"We paid gold to buy peace, but the price just rose.

We had no luck from the paths that we chose.

Clerics and scribes do not know what to do.

But, our mothers told us to summon you."

MICHAEL

"We do not like being servants at all.

In due time any master must soon fall.

We dislike Byzantines, Normans and Turks.

Not even Arab or Midi rule works."

STELLA

"Souls of aligned stones make and keep us free.

Honor is the roots of the cedar tree.

Fairness is the crystal spring to quench thirst.

Faith elevates the best over the worst."

FIDELIA

"We will seek to serve all in such manner.

We will not rule under any banner.

Allah, Jehovah and Lord are each God.

We till the mind, heart, humors, soul and sod."

FIERU

"Family comes first, then those that we know.

Next those over whose fate we do control.

We will know us by the place of our home.

It shines greater than the glory of Rome."

MICHAEL

"Praise God that we have truly chosen well.

It is time, of course, that surely will tell.

Their tact in judgement should pave the new way.

Their judgment in tactics may sway the day."

Mt. Liban – 1107 CE

MICHAEL

"The last two years show that our plan was right.

Our springs have names and our souls display might.

We have fights as any family will do.

But they resolve before the year is through."

YUSUF

"Yet, I fear that our plan may see its end.

Just as light through a crystal will bend.

A messenger soon arrives for them this day.

With such orders that may take them away."

JACAPO

"You have kept in touch although you did roam.

We have news of Daimbert's appeal to Rome.

He was wrongly disposed two years past.

His return was a sure die that was cast."

VINCENTE

"He would need his full guard on his return.

There are many grievous traitors to burn.

He has surely shown that he had not lied.

Unfortunately, he was sick and died."

JACAPO

"I do not have orders for you today.

Except, you may leave now without delay.

Return home to your own village and town.

Be glad you have set the world upside down."

VINCENTE

"Another visitor came with us here.

He fought some Turks near Haifa without fear.

He left after us so he will be late.

He must be here to contend with his fate."

NIOLO

"A father has no right to be so proud.

But, I must speak before I see death's shroud.

A mazzera saw my boar die too soon.

She saw me die before the next blue moon."

YUSUF

"The next blue moon appears quickly this night.

It will soon be out of our arc of sight.

Through your true daughters you were always here.

You need not worry at all now or fear."

NIOLO

"Know that you need to just trust your own heart.

It is from there that all honor will start.

I let hubris cloud my eyes not to see.

You are home now when you are fair and free."

MICHAEL

"Let them be alone as one in this hour.

Let this be joyful right now and not dour.

I believe the maquis' bouquet arrives.

It animates us all as hope survives."

STELLA

"Leave me fifty men and be on your way.

Return to your communes and towns this day.

The are crops to plant and ships to unload.

Your feet belong on your own pass or road."

FIDELIA

"Father has died and looks to you to lead.

He and mother left us wisdom to heed.

I should stay so you can take your true place.

It is your role for you to embrace."

STELLA

"I will lead now before it is too late.

You shall lead the commune to meet your fate.

Fieru must leave for trade pumps our heart.

The coast must build links to Jaffa to start."

FIERU

"I love you and will not leave you behind.

You are our breath and are one of a kind.

I would rather die than establish trade.

We three are bricks in the foundation laid."

STELLA

"Because I love you too, I act this way.

I must defer my love without delay.

Take the boar's baton and the honor too.

Travel from this home to your own home true."

Eight Pisan Ships Sail Toward Cyprus for Aleria – 1107 CE

FIDELIA

"Our troops look to us on this long sea trip.

Waves attack the fragile form of each ship.

We brace up and down as oak cracks in rhyme.

Our foe is not the Moors but slothful time."

FIERU

"Wait, black sails appear where they should not be.

This has been a Genoese controlled sea.

But there are sixteen ships on a fast course.

This is not a time for fear or remorse."

PISAN CAPTAIN

"They outnumber us at least two to one.

We will form two lines ahead of the Sun.

But they will try to split us from the pack.

They know that it is numbers we still lack."

"MOORISH" CAPTAIN

"We have four ships to your one ship alone.

Your God now gives you a chance to atone.

Give us her and the baton in your hand.

And, we will let your men swim to the land."

FIDELIA

"You did not bring enough men this day.

You may surely retreat without delay.

We stand as one firm tree that will not brake.

Your head will perch high on our shortest stake."

"MOORISH" CAPTAIN

"We did not come to debate, but to kill.

We shall kill him with such Saracen skill.

Take the baton and throw them overboard.

She will drown with him praying to her Lord."

PISAN SUB-COMMANDER

"Their ships left in flight as fast as they came.

It was almost as if it were a game.

They stole the baton, but they did not fight.

They did not use the full strength of their might."

PISAN CAPTAIN

"They blocked us from defending our lead boat.

They did not attack me, but did gloat.

Get her out of the water right away.

Or else she will soon drown in the salt spray."

PISAN SAILOR

"She is heavy and very hard to lift.

I will need some help as the waves will shift.

There are two bodies tied with rope as one.

It will take time for this task to be done."

FIDELIA

"Fieru just died trying to save me.

The baton was lost to keep us all free.

Let us sail fast to find our just revenge.

They must feel the pain of Hell fire's singe."

PISAN CAPTAIN

"We lack the ships for vengeance or power.

They will find stronger ships within the hour.

We are in the middle of a vast Sea.

Without supplies to find where they may be."

FIDELIA

"You are correct so steer us a course west.

Your words are very wise and serve us best.

His journey ends, as he is laid to rest.

To find the baton now will be my quest."

PISAN CAPTAIN

"I have sailed these seas all of my long life.

I know the skills, the joy, the pain and strife.

Yet, I have not seen Moors sail in that way.

Or not take slaves as part of any fray."

FIDELIA

"I will avenge his and the baton's loss.

I swear on my soul and this solemn cross.

The thieves and all of their blood kin shall die.

There will be none as they die to cry."

PISAN CAPTAIN

"We will soon land at Mariana's dock.

You will be as strong as the port's hard rock.

You will be a true leader we all need.

On your heavy heart we will all be freed."

Fidelia Travels from Mariana to the Niolo Valley – 1107 CE

MAYOR OF MARIANA

"We welcome these pilgrims returning home.

Let them never again have to leave or roam.

There is food, drink and rest as they may need.

There is no true thanks for their noble deed."

FIDELIA

"We honor the death of a brave native son.

Who honored this town with victories won.

He was always forthright, honest and fair.

He and my sister had no life to share."

FIERU'S FATHER

"I know he did just what he had to do.

Life only offers that chance to a few.

He was the port and the trade that it brought.

Trade must flourish with the freedom he bought."

FIDELIA

"We will find those who fast stole his young life.

Causing his family such pain and such strife.

But, I must return to my village soon.

I will hone faith in the light of the Moon."

MAYOR OF MARIANA

"Pilgrims suffer a lot for their small gain.

They lose friends in the dust, sand, pain and rain.

But, they become leaders to help us all.

That it why the young will answer the call."

FIDELIA

"I know this narrow path cut hard in stone.

It would be easy to fall down alone.

I approach the sole spring where life still sings.

I know its name and the hope that it brings."

YOUNG COUNT CINARCA

"My father is right that this spring is a weir.

Luscious women appear here without fear.

I will just wait to find a new conquest.

The next one is more pleasing than the rest."

FIDELIA

"Come here young count and feel my tight breast.

Does your mind now roam dreaming of the rest?

That my knife cuts your throat is a just gift.

To salve my sister from your father's rift."

FIDELIA'S MOTHER

"A Corsican woman returns in deed.

Your sister taught a girl much that you need.

I am old and cannot act any more.

You must act to build, yet even the score."

FIDELIA

"But, is this a good example to make?

That a leader can cut and make bones break?

Will I find the honor that vengeance brings?

And more judgment of tact over gold rings?"

Stella, Michael and Gregory Lead a Patrol to Protect Pilgrims on the Path Near the Border with the County of Tripoli – 1110 CE

MICHAEL

"Stella was right three years ago to say.

That we should patrol the true pilgrims' way.

Trade goes on smoothly with less bribes to pay.

Pilgrims can complete their pure path to pray."

GREGORY

"Emirs and counts like the money commerce brings.

Trips to a shrine means trade in holy things.

We can keep watch for those who mean us harm.

We can defend by sounding an alarm."

YUSUF

"Arabs still think the Franks are rude and loud.

The Franks say Arabs are effete and proud.

Yet, Arabs dislike Turks more than the Franks.

They will ally for power and trade ranks."

STELLA

"Emirs and counts have to act as they must.

They all seek the same power, fame and lust.

They are same in the East or in the West.

That is why we find freedom serves us best."

MICHAEL

"The Eastern Churches have seen this for years.

The leaders change, but not the flow of tears.

We worship Christ or pray five times each day.

Yet, we are worthless unless we can pay."

GREGORY

"I see a yellow cross on a red flag.

Thirty men in mail make the horses drag.

It is Count Bertrand and the royal host.

Riding here in form from Tripoli's coast."

COUNT BERTRAND OF TRIPOLI

"Stella, why do you not become my wife.

I can take you away from all this strife.

Why not ally your tribes under my care?

I am a count that is both just and fair."

STELLA

"Saying you are just does not make it true.

Your cousin William may differ with you.

Is there real peace within your county wide?

Why then should we now align with your side?"

COUNT BERTRAND OF TRIPOLI

"A remote cousin of Mawdud heads this way.

She goes to pray in the City this day.

New pilgrims from France arrive here next week.

Looking for straggler Moors who appear weak."

YUSUF

"The pilgrim's path seeks peace within the fight.

Battles are heard but remain out of sight.

We patrol and protect Frank, Turk or Moor.

We rebuff petulant counts, sheiks and more."

Stella, Michael and Gregory Observe an Encounter Between Reynald, a Recent Pilgrim from the West, and the Muslim Caravan of Zahra and Her Precocious Daughter Fatima – 1110 CE

STELLA

"It has been a week since Bertrand was here.

A very rich caravan draws very near.

Act as a shadow does to greet the night.

I feel that we surely will have a fight."

ZAHRA

"I feel safe now, but I do not know why.

The dust cakes on our skin making it dry.

We will stop soon as our men will need rest.

Our trip to the Great Mosque may be a test."

FATIMA

"I walk barefoot to show my faith inside.

Even when the mufti keeps me outside.

I need no mufti to know who I am.

I am a young independent woman."

ZAHRA

"Your wise comments belie such a young face.

Your mind explores at its own time and pace.

But, this journey must now find the next well.

Or else, hunger and thirst wields their own tale."

FATIMA

"Why does a storm gather from swirling dust?

What omens arise that we soon can trust?

I will draw near to help safekeep our guards.

My own fortune still remains in the cards."

REYNALD

"I find captives on my very first quest.
You will find that my horsemen are the best.
You will fetch a fine ransom after we lie.
Some rash emir will not want you to die."

ZAHRA

"We pass at Baldwin's will and oath of care.
We are pilgrims not slaves sold at some fair.
There is a pact that promotes faith and trade.
It protects us from your ignoble raid."

REYNALD

"Baldwin is king because of his past deeds.
He is fair, but attends to his own needs.
He gives too much sway to the Eastern way.
He will soon have the greatest price to pay."

FATIMA

"You are a speck of dirt in our true path.
You will feel the weight of my uncle's wrath.
Leave us and we will forget you this day.
There is now little left for us to say."

REYNALD

"I am not blind to what I see around.
Your uncle will pay for what I have found.
You should lie nude like the whores that you are.
Your soul screams will sound very near and far."

STELLA

"Back away quickly or die where to stand.

Step aside and take a sword in your hand.

Your host is captive leaving you alone.

I hope my blade allows you to atone."

REYNALD

"I need no help to beat you with my knife.

I will bed them after I take your life.

Come near so we start this fight as we might.

I want to leave before day becomes night."

STELLA

"You parry before this combat should start.

You strike me in the ribs below my heart.

Never mind now as your head will soon fall.

My sword shakes as it answers God's cold call."

ZAHRA

"I did not know a man could run so fast.

He seeks to avoid his blood and his past.

Your strength shows that we have little to fear.

Yet, I do not know you from around here."

FATIMA

"St. Lucy's eye lays so still on her chest.

She must be from the isle of rock out West.

That old pendant shows she has come so far.

She shines with the stone as a guiding star."

MICHAEL

"We will escort you to King Baldwin's land.

They will await you with a cohort grand.

Praise be to God you are now safe and sound.

And that there was no blood spilt on the ground."

GREGORY

"This may be the last time we meet this way.

New drumbeats of jihad shake the long day.

Ships with kings and new zealots soon arrive.

I do not know how we will survive."

ZAHRA

"No words express our true thanks to you all.

Your deeds resound in tale long to recall.

My brother will be told what you have done.

He too will give thanks for life that is won."

FATIMA

"I now know more than muftis could ever teach.

Pride lives close within the scope of my reach.

Fairness and faith are wealth beyond compare.

Fealty to oaths must be like breathing air."

STELLA

"We can only do what we can and know.

I am a Corsican with pain to show.

Let us make the trip before it is night.

Reynald may return looking for a fight."

MICHAEL

"The three-day trip to the border now ends.

We hope all camps heed the message it sends.

We head home so we can repeat this act.

That we co-exist, yet still hate, is fact."

GREGORY

"Banners and titles are façades we make.

They are an excuse for rulers to fake.

Yet, they walk barefoot to remit their sin.

And their God favors them with a key win."

YUSUF

"We serve the same God, but are hurt the same.

Our rites and prayers differ to great blame.

Servants of your Christ kill their own the worst.

Arabs will maim and attack the Turk first."

STELLA

"We must look at the whole and not the parts.

Life is complex and that is where it starts.

Except, I know that peace dwells in my springs.

Water salves and solves all issues life brings."

MICHAEL

"That is why you name the springs as you do.

We will wait for your return with the dew.

We are links in a strong unbroken chain.

That binds us all as one in love and pain."

The Cycle of Cyrnos
On the Return from Escorting Zahra
Stella Encounters Tajik Al Jabbar, Brother and Uncle Respectively
to Zahra and Fatima at Stella's Springs

STELLA

"You flow true like the springs I knew back home.

You will make me stay here and never roam.

My wound heals slowly with the water's touch.

This is tranquil even though I hurt so much."

TAJIK AL JABBAR

"Does your house not have is own warm tile bath?

To soothe your soul's song from the daily wrath?

I feel your sharp pain though there are no cries.

Let me come near while I avert my eyes."

STELLA

"These springs welcome all to take a long drink.

I wear all my clothes as I sit and think.

You can approach now if you seek to dare.

Whether you live or die is not my care."

TAJIK AL JABBAR

"You were there for my sister and my niece.

When some rogue thought they were the golden fleece.

My respect saves you from any abuse.

Fall into sleep and do not be obtuse."

KAREEM, CAPTAIN OF THE HOUSE OF TAJIK AL JABBAR

"We will take her now to your house this night.

I fear this one though may be ready to fight.

Her care will the highest that we can give.

We will spare no expense for her to live."

51

TAJIK AL JABBAR

"Your skin glistens like I have never seen.

Sheer gossamer clings to a form so clean.

Yet, I just see your wounds that need repair.

My Muslim doctors can give the best care."

STELLA

"Reynald's knife blade cut a deep gash and tear.

Yet, you only give me some veil to wear.

Our healers may not use art and oil.

But, they apply family tack and toil."

TAJIK AL JABBAR

"I thought science would spur you to know more.

Rather than to repeat rote tales and lore.

But, I made you a suit stronger than mail.

Go change and feel what the fabric may tell."

STELLA

"This is a great gift from God beyond compare.

The fabric is strong yet lighter than air.

I can move like I have no clothes at all.

No blade will cut flesh if I flex or fall."

TAJIK AL JABBAR

"My wives fear the figure that you suggest.

They sense that they no longer are the best.

Yet, I clothe you for your mission next week.

You will need it for the goal that you seek."

STELLA

"Why do you speak in such cold cryptic words?

Do your wizards need to augur some birds?

The damask weave invests a fighter's skill.

To foster full peace and not some random kill."

TAJIK AL JABBAR

"We share farms, trade and the same stars at night.

We respect each other, yet we still fight.

Do you know why we hate the Frankish brand?

It is because you have taken our land!"

STELLA

"We have taken only what you took first.

The taking does not make us best or worst.

How we use what we take is the true test.

Those who were here take no comfort in rest."

TAJIK AL JABBAR

"You are a child of the mountains so cold.

You dislike emirs, counts, silver and gold.

Pisa opens trade with the Romans through here.

They ally with us for profits so clear."

STELLA

"Yes, we leave next week to open the way.

Then head back West among the salt sea spray.

Let us feast on local foods on display.

As we may fight each other the next day."

The Return to Niolo Valley – 1112 CE

YOUNG COUNT GANELON

"These springs are where the young Cinarca fell.

A victim of careless lust at this well.

We will not make the same poor mistake.

Hold her fast, as I enjoy what I can take."

STELLA

"Touch my sister and each of you will die.

Your heads will fall without a sound or cry.

My old debt to honor remains intact.

But will be made whole with a single act."

MICHAEL

"My welcome is the grace of the warm rains

Let the Pisan troops arrest them in chains.

I must drink from water so clean and pure.

Remit my sins back East with a true cure."

FIDELIA

"I did not need your help to win the day.

You both must imbibe now with no delay.

We must gather and hold the greatest feast.

My sister and love arrive from the East."

CAPTAIN OF THE PISAN GUARD

"Let us be gone and out of your way.

You three have so much more to feel and say.

These four thugs will rot in the darkest cell.

They will regret their short time at this well."

STELLA

"I feel like I never did leave the place.

Fairness and freedom live in time and space.

We are here to build with stones of the past.

Our free foundation that will always last."

FIDELIA

"Your suit is so sleek and singles you out.

It shows such skill and strength dismissing doubt.

The counts will face a new formidable foe.

But there are flocks to herd and crops to sow."

MICHAEL

"You two will lead wherever you may be.

You fuel the fragile fulcrum to be free.

My home burns from fires of Turkish zeal.

It is a loss of my own soul so real."

STELLA

"You gave us a home when we were so lost.

We brought new burdens adding to your cost.

You will be here where we will share our bed.

We can return home years after we wed."

FIDELIA

"We shall feast for your marriage and return.

Let the mutton braise and the fires burn.

Trade, intrigue and battles may cross the Sea.

But, true balance beckons all things to be."

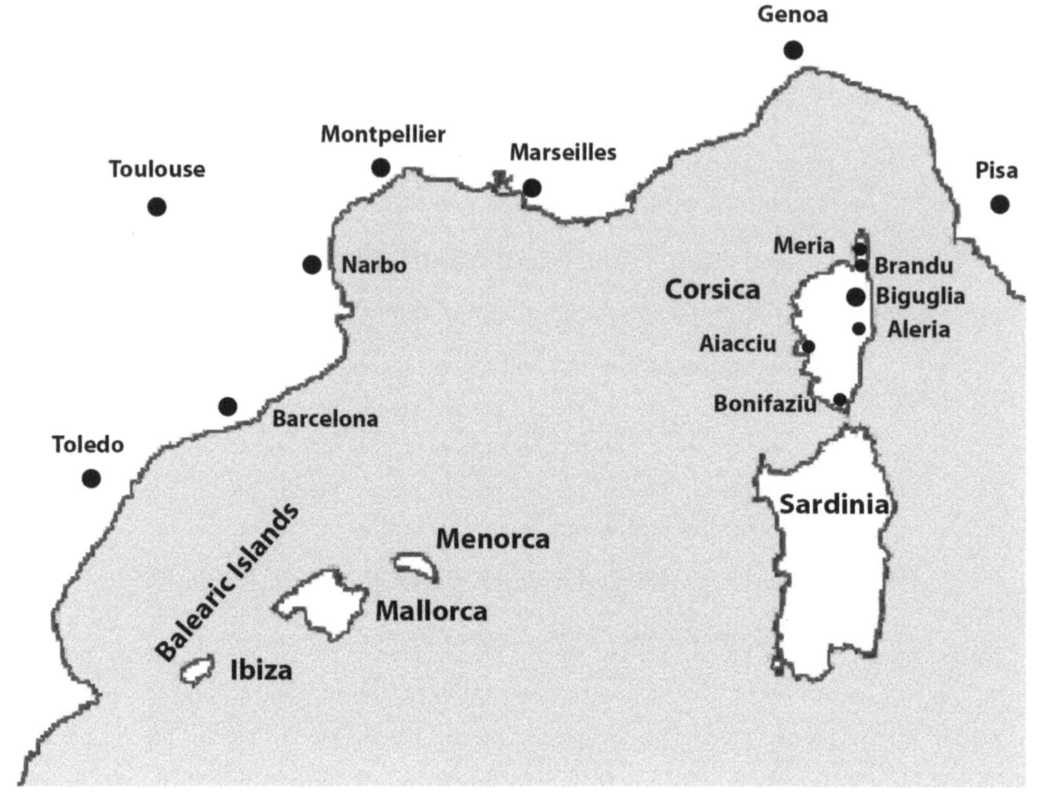

Genoa
Montpellier
Marseilles
Toulouse
Pisa
Meria
Brandu
Narbo
Corsica
Biguglia
Aliacciu
Aleria
Bonifaziu
Toledo
Barcelona
Sardinia
Balearic Islands
Menorca
Mallorca
Ibiza

Aquitane
Genoa
Toulouse
Pisa
Marseilles
Narbo
Navarre
Rome
Tortosa
Barcelona
Toledo
Grenada
Almeria
Almohads

Pisa Enlists Corsicans to Join the Catalan-Pisan-Provençal Rescue of Occupied Ibiza – 1114 CE

FIDELIA

"What town are you from and who do you know?

You come from the coast like a clever crow.

Do you know why we live up here so high?

To be far from trouble yet near the sky."

HECTOR

"I am from Luri and I knew Fieru.

I am his brother that he never knew.

I accept the Cross and profess my quest.

To those who truly knew him at his best."

STELLA

"This crow knows such words to tempt us to leave.

We have what he wants, but we cannot believe.

I left the cross three years hence for this home.

My duty is here with no time to roam."

BISHOP OF MARIANA

"You have been fighting the Moors in the West.

Four hundred years have gone with little rest.

Before, duty drove you to fight the Moors.

Now, the cross targets Moors beyond your shores."

COUNT RAYMOND OF BARCELONA

"I invoke the oaths of three thousand years.

The strength of our bonds is not in arrears.

Our ports trade not clay pots but deathly fears.

We must strike the Muslim base creating tears."

STELLA

"But, all I see are more counts seeking war.

This is not the free-men trading as before.

We see flags of which count rise over the walls.

To signal who owns the city that falls."

HECTOR

"You truly see that image in your mind.

It holds you fast to a truth left behind.

But, is there honor left for you to find?

I may have a clue of the tie that binds."

FELIX

"There was a lading bill for the lost boar.

Stating where it will be after that war.

We bought part which I hope was not a trick.

So, we hope and pray you read Arabic."

MICHAEL

"It sails West on course with the gales and guile.

To where there have been designs on the isle.

The pirates are not true but are mock Moors.

They go to a half-Celtic land of yore."

FIDELIA

"The quest sails West in need of winds and skill.

The Balearics are base for war at will.

Its Taifa is Moor in name, but not faith.

Its Celtic past lurks like a fog-like wraith."

STELLA

"My sister leads without care for her life.

Yet, her burden weighs heavy with such strife.

I believe these words are contrived and fake.

And have the meanings she who listens make."

MICHAEL

"The text describes the southern French coast.

Or, the Tuscan Sea where pirates still boast.

But, we must trust her and sail this next day.

Chasing the boar is a price we must pay."

COUNT RAYMOND OF BARCELONA

"Our hearts differ, but our goal is the same.

The cross suffuses our purpose and our name.

All the south of France deploys this fortnight.

We join them and the Pisan fleet to fight."

BISHOP OF MARIANA

"Five pillars buttress such a righteous cause.

The devil Moors will soon tremble and pause.

We will rid the scourge from the northwest Sea.

Making all of our lands fertile and free."

FIDELIA

"The riddle knew me to call my sole quest.

My answer means that only I go West.

I last saw the baton in my full sight.

My duty calls, not yours, to make this right."

The Crusade to the Balearic Islands of Ibiza and Majorca – 1114 CE

STELLA

"Did you think we would leave you on your own?

Your fictive guilt festers while it has grown.

You built the village beyond all compare.

We will remove this worn weight if you dare."

FIDELIA

"Michael and you have a young son to rear.

He needs his mother to allay each fear.

Fieru is gone and cannot help out.

Only I can resolve the pain and doubt."

MICHAEL

"Paolo seeks freedom from the chains of age.

He needs to find how to channel his rage.

At two, his life seeks to make its own start.

He is so stubborn, but is very smart."

PISAN CAPTAIN

"We sail one-hundred twenty ships in rows.

A like number follow for strength that shows.

The pirates have skill and will leave the port.

They will withdraw and make us siege their fort."

BISHOP OF MARIANA

"The withdraw as they know God makes us win.

The saints join us for remission of sins.

Legates have long found the call of the cross.

Helping Spanish counts reconquest their loss."

Stella, Fidelia, Michael and Hector Approach and Deploy on the Beaches of Ibiza – 1115 CE

STELLA

"Grasp any harder and the ship's wood will break.

Your pain calls as if your life is at stake.

You are like Greek fire with such a short fuse.

You seek to burn bright as part of this ruse."

FIDELIA

"How can you pretend they play on my fear?

When the object of my quest is so near.

I share your fire for the fight inside.

I too find fealty supplants all pride."

MICHAEL

"No one contests you are true to your word.

Your faith and skill will stand out from the herd.

The clues though are plain, but vague and obscure.

They comprise a strong inescapable lure."

STELLA

"There will be no battle for us to fight.

They have no answer for our ships and might.

Our sails will signal their time to withdraw.

They will leave when the craven crow may caw."

FIDELIA

"Then, we must find them where they try to hide.

They cannot escape the force of our side.

We are dogs chasing the fox from a lair.

We remit our sins without a prayer."

HECTOR

"Come now before the others will deploy.

This is not the time to be slow or coy.

They hide in caves with the baton in tow.

This is the one chance that fate did bestow."

FIDELIA

"How do you know fortune deems these facts true?

Did you observe some close movement or clue?

How many must help us assault each cave?

This is the time for the action we crave."

HECTOR

"There is a spy who is now rich in gold.

These are the facts which we have now been told.

The approach is narrow with steep stone walls.

It takes two in single file as fate calls."

FIDELIA

"Do you know in which cave the baton rests?

Or does each cave offer us a new test?

Must we be worthy to fulfill this quest?

Must we show that our true faith is the best?"

HECTOR

"I know the cave and the true path to take.

You are honest while the others are fake.

I will follow you, but ten steps behind.

Just in case it is trouble that we find."

FIDELIA

"I feel less like the hunter than the prey.

I am caught in this gauntlet's narrow way.

What is that cascading crash and sound?

Why has Hector run not to be found?"

COUNT GANELON'S MIDDLE SON

"She will soon crouch down and be all alone.

This is the time she must pay and atone.

Aim for her head to silence her now.

Use naphtha to burn the flesh of this cow."

FIDELIA

"I fell into this trap with my eyes shut.

Blood covers my hubris with each flesh cut.

I cannot attack from this open space.

I soon join Fieru at a fast pace."

COUNT RAYMOND OF BARCELONA

"Stella's sister has received Judas' kiss.

She lives a duel that death cannot dismiss.

Thirty men soon rescue her from her plight.

I did not endorse this brand of false fight."

CATALAN CAPTAIN

"Flush them from their perch along the short mile.

May Ganelon's spawn choke on their own bile.

She is not Roland to die from deceit.

She will see their blood flow from wounds discrete."

STELLA

"Sister, why did you begin without me?

Why did you leave us on ships on the sea?

We will be there until your quest is done.

We will stand as one when the war is won."

MICHAEL

"Hector was paid well to tell you a lie.

To ambush you until you would soon die.

Hector will want to ponder his short pay.

As he hangs from a rope dead this fine day."

COUNT RAYMOND OF BARCELONA

"The baton will be found in your due time.

It will not yield to their vile, heinous crime.

You will have my troops at your beck and call.

You will not lack from my support at all."

STELLA

"Our oath does no end as this island falls.

The Moors withdraw within Majorca's walls.

We join the siege to complete this brief war.

We will watch as your banners will soar."

FIDELIA

"My quest now is empty and I am lost.

Your oath is a prize that lessens the cost.

Let us win with the song a victor sings.

Then, we will leave to find our village springs."

BOOK TWENTY

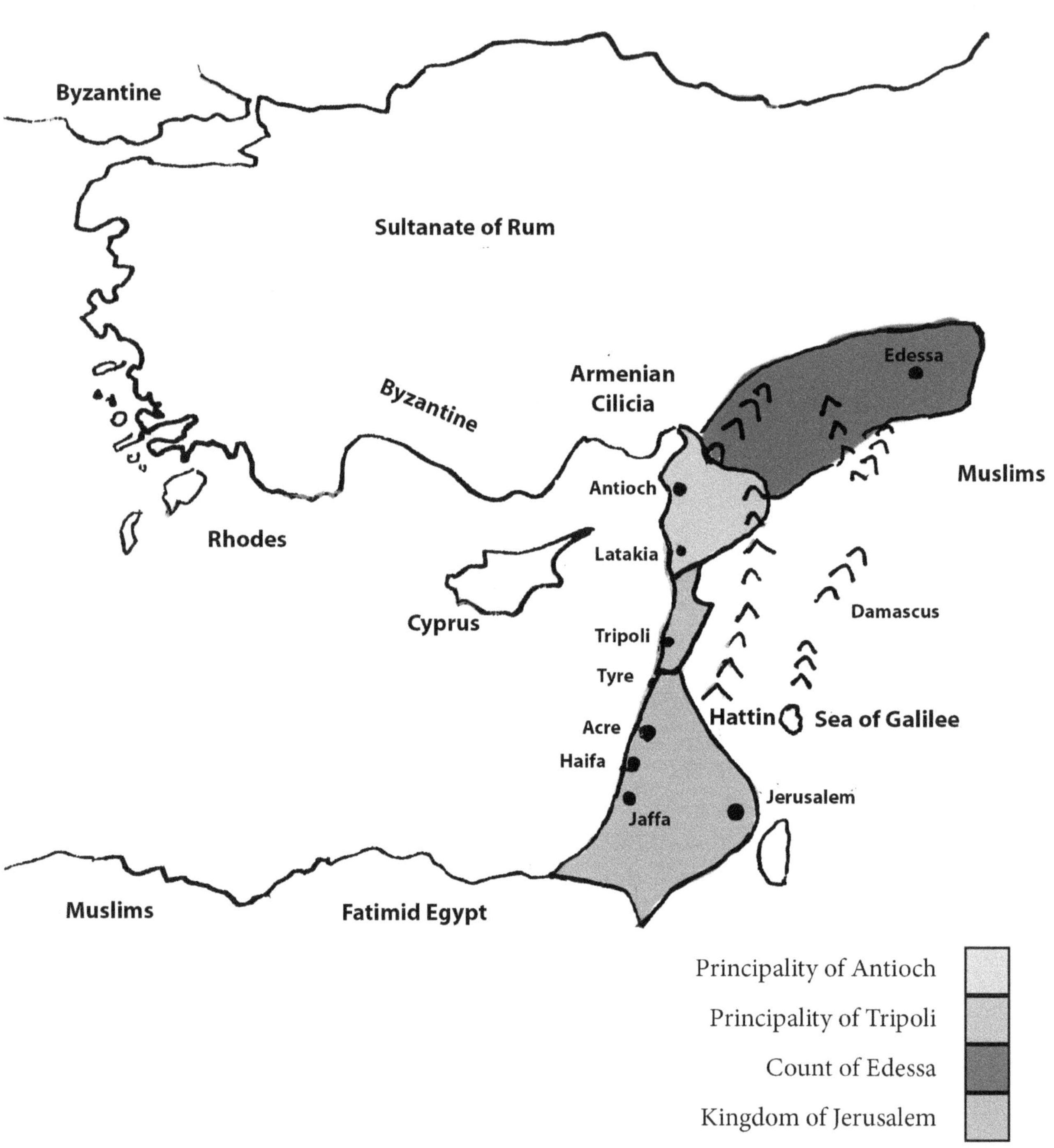

Outremer – The Latin Kingdoms after the First Crusade – 1120 CE

The Medieval Quintet: Regeneration 1115-1215 CE

TASH

"Solace is sometimes very hard to find.

Displaced trust can frustrate the ties that bind.

Elastic culture though can cure all woes.

Fixing faith against its formidable foes."

PATTI

"Moors erupt like a furtive seismic blast.

Stealing a new wife, yet leaving so fast.

This slave will soon master her new emir.

They will learn the full face of a new fear."

BERNADETTE

"The search for the baton finds a new band.

Honor is cast for the heart of the land.

Travel is made to an original time.

A path lost to current measure and rhyme."

MARY

"Envy is a white-hot coal in a flame.

Searing the Genoese soul without shame.

The isle is too rich to escape its sphere.

Stealth moves enhance and stoke Pisa's fear."

CHARLOTTE

"The counts are a vise hoping freemen break.

The guidance of the commune is at stake.

But, freedom is reprieved by an old host.

Fairness and justice still matter most."

Stella, Fidelia and Michael Return to Niolo Valley – 1115 CE

STELLA

"This seems like an odyssey after war.

Unlike trips to and from Narbo before.

This three-day passage passes like a year.

With no exchange of goods in this trade sphere."

MICHAEL

"Yet, the waves reveal a stone shore in sight.

With horses we will see our son tonight.

Our twelve-month trip will soon come to an end.

We will find a true dock 'round the next bend."

FIDELIA

"The dusk shows us home and you to your son.

I seek the spring and to my own peace won.

But wait now, stones stand and surround the spout.

I may not drink to salve my pain, no doubt."

LA DONNA DELLA SIGNORA

"The spring brought you to save them and not cry.

In your absence, fairness and trust ran dry.

You have no sins to remit or faith lost.

Stella and you were needed at all cost."

IL MAZZERO

"The valley has restored faith as it must.

But it needs action to show how to trust.

Your cousin broke his oath without regret.

Here is his story we will not forget."

At an Assembly of Podesti in the Niolo Valley After Stella, Fidelia and Michael Leave for the Balearic Crusade – 1114 CE

TRADISCE

"My cousins have left to fight for the Cross.

Their absence will leave us with a great loss.

But we must live as if they were still here.

We cannot concede contempt or our fear."

GHJURAMENTU

"You are the oldest member of your clan.

Which for years has led with grace and élan.

Striving to be true, fair and just for all.

Keeping us well beyond the counts' bile pall."

DEBULE

"Do we need to hear more to do our job?

This is order over the lawless mob.

Let us proclaim our leader without haste.

More words would simply be a worthless waste."

VAL

"Yes, he has not said the oath he must take.

With such words that are true and far from fake.

I have not heard the plans he will pursue.

To lift us up all and not just a few."

TRADISCE

"Put your faith in me and not let it sway.

Trust that I will soon show you the way.

Those that do not support us will be foes.

I do not need to hear of any woes."

GHJURAMENTU

"I have just now come from the valley's spring.

Stones block access and the life that it brings.

Quickly, you broke your oath like none before.

What more heinous harm do we have in store?

TRADISCE

"I cannot break that which I did not take.

But, I have many more measures to make.

I have brought order my cousins could not.

Faith in me found the lost greatness we sought."

DEBULE

"The counts will soon take your detractors' land.

Without our help, they cannot make a stand.

I have brought Val in cold chains as we must.

She refused to come or grant you her trust."

VAL

"You took an oath as part of your own plan

You did that, as you became head of the clan.

We will defy you until you will fall.

Then fairness returns to benefit all."

TRADISCE

"Quiet woman, you will become my wife.

You will please me to release all my strife.

Make her virtue bow and beg on one knee.

When she will succumb, then she can be free."

DEBULE

"Your rage explodes as she defies you still.
Seven months have not broken her strong will.
Her village vows vengeance to cure your harm.
Allies join to respond to her alarm."

TRADISCE

"She dishonors me, yet they plot with her.
I will crush those that ally with this cur.
I will grant succor to those who like me.
This is the fair way that just has to be."

IL MAZZERO

"I have had a dream where I saw you die.
I chased a boar as gray as the dusk sky.
You will pass within four months from this date.
Nothing will change or prevent this sure fate."

GHJURAMENTU

"The valley has a sure message to send.
You may break me, but you must fear your end.
Culture cannot prevail under your rule.
It suffers neither hubris nor a fool."

TRADISCE

"I will find this gray boar and kill it first.
Its blood will honor me and quench my thirst.
Old magic cannot hasten my demise.
I will, in turn, supply my own surprise."

DEBULE

"Four months have gone with no gray boar in sight.

The valley still trembles with further fright.

Your troops chase a pig that may not exist.

Your foes ally and combine to resist."

TRADISCE

"They will suffer pain when I soon return.

Their faith will soon rot and their crops will burn.

There is the gray boar within our own sight.

Kill it now absorbing its fulsome might."

GHJURAMENTU

"You return with your prize laid on the ground.

Yet, you fail to fathom the fee you found.

You still will pay for the harm you have done.

In the end, it is the boar that has won."

TRADISCE

"You fool, how can you say that I will lose.

I have shown my own true fate I can choose.

This boar begs in its own black blood so thick.

I am the master as shown by my kick."

IL MAZZERO

"Do not kick a boar which still has its tusk.

He bled from his foot and was dead by dusk.

The valley is now back where it should be.

Ready for fair and just guides to be free."

LA DONNA DELLA SIGNORA

"You two were drawn back to your proper place.

Like your father to bring peace to this space.

The baton was never within your reach.

These are lessons the village had to teach."

IL MAZZERO

"I walk through many dreams at the same time.

I move with the forms, the shades and the rhyme.

None of you appear as prey to be found.

You belong here to protect the stone ground."

FIDELIA

"Crush the stone wall from the spring and spout.

Let peace pour for all and me without doubt.

We go to each village to list their needs.

Bringing with us vines, ewes, cows, sows and seeds."

STELLA

"We will reclaim all our land from our foe.

The counts will not bestow any more woe.

The commune will bolster our due defense.

Our bonds will be as strong as any fence."

MICHAEL

"We are grateful to have this humble quest.

We welcome the chance to overcome this test.

These plains are gems of a value untold.

The layers of gifts have yet to unfold."

Pascal Paul Piazza

Enrico O Arrigo of Accia and Albertus of Genoa Address Pope Innocent II
Over the Appointment of Bishops in Corsica – 1133 CE

ENRICO

"Pisa names all six bishops on the isle.

It thus controls the Church's profits and style.

Dogma was strong in each village and town.

But empty mitres turn that upside down."

ALBERTUS

"Pisans are merchants afraid to act fast.

Their caution keeps them stuck in their own past.

Genoese ships seek more than new trade rights.

The Pope will expand its coffers and rites."

POPE INNOCENT III

"Why should I change when Pisa has done well?

Facts ring out like the peal of a bronze bell.

Liguria lusts for an open door.

Three bishops will just fuel a taste for more."

ALBERTUS

"Prior popes put Pisa in place for good.

But its sloth spoils the wax, resin and wood.

We need faithful traders to fight the Moors.

Yes, we ask you to open the shut door."

POPE INNOCENT II

"We must honor pilgrims who put faith first.

To close our hearts and minds invites the worst.

You shall now have your foothold that you ask.

Naming three of six bishops is your task."

Boethius Attracts a Pisan Flotilla Assembled Off of Aleria – 1147 CE

BOETHIUS

"Where are the trade ships that would dock this day?

There are debts to Provence and Narbo to pay.

Pisan ships project their crosses with pride.

Where will sixty war ships sail with the tide?

GHJUDICE – PISAN BISHOP OF ALERIA

"Let us dock, drink and discuss as we meet.

The Pope commands the mission of this fleet.

The Pisan host charts a course to the West.

A true bearing to reconquest the rest."

LUIGI D'ORO – PISAN CAPTAIN

"Edessa has fallen on Christmas Day.

We must respond in a compelling way.

Louis and Conrad shall invade the East.

Northern knights seek to slay the Wendish beast."

GHJUDICE – PISAN BISHOP OF ALERIA

"Where are those who ran to old Urban's call?

Why have they gone and let Edessa fall?

Pilgrims go West to lose all their sins.

As will those whose profits fill the trade bins."

LUIGI D'ORO – PISAN CAPTAIN

"We invest docks where the Moor mostly trades.

Almeria will choke on blood from our blades.

The Maghreb explodes so the reserves stall."

The absence of new troops foretell their fall."

The Combined Catalan-Provencal-Pisan Fleet Joins the Siege of Almeria – 1147 CE

RAYMOND IV - COUNT OF BARCELONA

"The Pisan ships join our host off the coast.

We could arrive like a trumpet's bold boast.

But, we must be silent as we deploy.

We are about to join an ambush ploy!"

WILLIAM - COUNT OF MONTPELLIER

"A small band of Moors will leave from their gate.

When they sense a trap it will be too late.

They should withdraw and accept their fate.

Most may die at a sad, alarming rate."

PONS - COUNT OF CABRERA (THE RUIN OF THE MOORS)

"The Moors have stolen much of God's own land.

We cannot let this great injustice stand.

We have a great gift to restore the peace.

We must return now the lost golden fleece."

ALFONSO - COUNT OF GALICIA

"I truly hate the Moors with lustful zeal.

War is peace for us and the threat they feel.

Devine wrath slays and stacks Moorish heads deep.

They will find their virgins under Death's sleep."

GHJUDICE - PISAN BISHOP OF ALERIA

"It took five months for Almeria to fall.

The carnage seems well beyond the Pope's call.

The full reconquest of Spain is on pace.

Boethius now must leave Death's own place."

Boethius Takes a Provencal Ship Which Arrives at the Port of Narbo
after the Fall of Almeria – 1148 CE

Provencal Captain

"I have not seen a sea of such solace!

Pure peaceful waves come from Neptune's palace.

Our reward is a fast trip to our homes.

Waves glisten like conquered Moorish domes."

GHJUDICE - PISAN BISHOP OF ALERIA

"The Provencal ship will drop you off soon.

Narbo's known harbor should dispel your swoon.

Lust for lucre led to a luster lost.

We must reconquest the Moors at all cost."

BOETHIUS

"I know the Moors took Spain's Christian soil.

Making us expend out blood, sweat and toil.

There should be less raids to menace our shores.

But after we win must we kill all Moors?"

ERMENGARD - VISCOUNTESS OF NARBO

"Old friends appear as we start on our quest.

Supply them with care and all our best.

Let us hear stories of war firm and fair.

Until the work-fire smoke clears the air."

ANTONIN - CORSICAN FRIEND OF BOETHIUS LIVING IN NARBO

"Why is my Corsican brother so sad.

If you do not smile my wife will be mad.

Join a feast like one you had as a child.

Fine figatelli and cheese pungent and mild."

Pascal Paul Piazza

**Boethius Eats at the Home of Antonin and Cecile and Discuss Ermengard
the Ruler of Narbo – 1148 CE**

BOETHIUS

"Who is she whose mail moves with fulsome grace?

Who hosts the brilliant Moon glow in her face?

You run the best docks in the south of France.

Even your clockwork succumbs to her trance."

ANTONIN

"We outfit her ships to sail when she asks.

We are never lost for challenging tasks.

Venus gave her beauty no one can test.

Except for Deb, she surpasses the rest."

CECILE

"Why do you men only see how she looks?

When she is a scholar of ancient books.

When she rules likewise Solomon of old.

Her skill with wisdom and sword are like gold."

ERMENGARD - VISCOUNTESS OF NARBO

"I do not deserve the comments you make.

I am lucky to have chances to take.

I need men who saw Almeria's walls fall.

We sail to invest Tortosa's high hall."

BOETHIUS

"The call of the cross will not reach my ears.

I am a lost insouciance of fears.

You speak with a faith that is firm and fair.

Yet, I have no more endless hope to spare."

ANTONIN

"We Corsicans know the pain that you feel.

You groan from the crush of the ethics heel.

But, Tortosa's docks will suffer from war.

You must help me rebuild them for ships to moor."

CECILE

"We are far from home and cannot be there.

But, you cannot displace faith with despair.

My husband is not a soldier at all.

I need you to see that he does not fall."

ERMENGARD - VISCOUNTESS OF NARBO

"Do you know the origin of your name?

Being a scholar was his claim to fame.

He found reason to build a moral life.

As salve to suppress all suffering strife."

BOETHIUS

"Flattery belies reason's main appeal.

My own mind must not just think, but feel.

I am honor bound too to join my friend.

Even if it means our death in the end."

ERMENGARD - VISCOUNTESS OF NARBO

"We need more to keep the oath as you do.

I will be there to honor its faith too.

The Catalans too are fervent and fair.

We will find a balm for all your pain there."

The Siege of Tortosa – 1148 CE

RAYMOND IV BERENGUER - COUNT OF BARCELONA

"There was a rash move by Genoese pikes.

Still, the outer walls fell with a few strikes.

The Moors withdrew behind true solid walls.

Will my troops disperse as the campaign stalls?"

ALBERTO OF GENOA

"We will be steady and fill in the moat.

We will attack like an old, stubborn goat.

It will take some months, but we cannot fail.

We find solace as they sweat in their jail."

ERMENGARD - VISCOUNTESS OF NARBO

"For five months their walls stand stable like Troy.

We too need a horse or a clever ploy.

Is there a plan that is novel and sage?

Or else, we too may succumb to blind rage."

WILLIAM - COUNT OF MONTPELLIER

"Their nobles propose an audacious pact.

Hoping we deploy some judgement of tact.

Their relief must arrive in forty days.

If not, then they will leave with the sun's rays."

GARCIA RAMIREZ IV - KING OF NAVARRE

"They pledge solid Moor hostages in good stead.

They want to live long and not end up dead.

When Asćo falls, there will be no relief.

We can live with true honor and belief."

ANTONIN

"Asćo fell and the relief troops withdrew.

The Moors kept their word when it became due.

The docks for war must be re-fit for trade.

The Ebro again will set the high grade."

BOETHIUS

"Trade links with the Ebro are long overdue.

The ancient sea routes will return as new.

We can honor the cross on true facts too.

Avoiding such painful choices we might soon rue."

WILLIAM - COUNT OF MONTPELLIER

"Only Narbo can restore the docks right.

Bringing wealth to all from this holy fight.

Monastic life is the next path for me.

Our flags in flight are a great sight to see."

ERMENGARD - VISCOUNTESS OF NARBO

"Our task is done if one Corsican stays.

It honors the true nature of your ways.

Can I entice my new friend to delay?

There will be new, old books to make you stay!"

RAYMOND IV BERENGUER - COUNT OF BARCELONA

"My flags waves high as a sign that we won.

Your skills and traits will get the new task done.

I cede free trade rights to Narbo without fail.

And a villa with its own spring fed well."

Ermengard Entertains Boethius in the Villa Narbonais – 1148 CE

ERMENGARD - VISCOUNTESS OF NARBO

"The Moor knows how to make fabric so sheer.

I can lounge in private peace without fear.

My soft auburn hair can fall to my hips.

I contemplate logic not war or ships."

BOETHIUS

"I must bathe before I wear these new robes.

I have dirt from my feet to my ear lobes.

I shall wash alone to keep myself clean.

It is hard to remove this dusty sheen."

ERMENGARD - VISCOUNTESS OF NARBO

"My henna tattoos are gone the next day.

But, they verify what the verse will say.

My sheer damask clings to my thigh and breast.

Your eyes disclose the line you like best."

BOETHIUS

"I read Occitan verse of Roland's text.

But, what are the symbols that appear next?

They are set as if in a magic spell.

I must touch each to know what they do tell."

ERMENGARD - VISCOUNTESS OF NARBO

"It is Euclid's prime that I have just read.

My books abound with me to make my bed.

Stay and run Narbo's harbor in this land.

There is knowledge here you must understand."

Boethius Returns to Narbo After the Five Year Task to Restore and Establish the Harbor of Tortosa – 1153 CE

BOETHIUS

"I hear that Tortosa has the best docks.

And Narbo is nothing but scattered rocks.

It has been the quick end of five short years.

The sea waves cry on our rocks with its tears."

ANTONIN

"Those are the words that you now have to say?

One night in bed is a high price to pay!

It is good to see you again my friend.

Are you off to home or to some new end?"

BOETHIUS

"My soul and her honor are still intact.

You should not take such rumors as true fact.

I was born into Ursu's line and pace.

The path to his birth home I will retrace."

CECILE

"I told you she had strength beyond her face.

She attacks wearing either mail or lace.

She won you over with her wit and charms.

There was solace surely in her sure arms."

ANTONIN

"I married a goddess in her own right.

Who rules my life both robust day and night.

Let us go and eat a feast she will make.

There are fresh figs to spread and bread to bake."

Boethius Arrives at the Same Springs in France Where Ursu First Met Clovis Before He Became King of the Franks and Which Now are Within the Domain of the Newly Married Henry Plantagenet of Anjou and Eleanor of Aquitaine and One Year Before Henry Becomes Henry II, King of England, Aquitaine, Normandy, Poitiers and Anjou – 1153 CE

BOETHIUS

"Why is your stance so stern and gaze so grim?

Have these springs dried out for this poor pilgrim?

I re-trace the trail that Ursu did take.

Here is where I have a life-choice to make."

HENRY OF ANJOU - COUNT OF NORMANDY

"Ursu fought with Arthur at Badon's Hill.

Anyone in the bear's line may drink his fill.

Ursu met young Clovis with his brash sword.

Before he was king and had heard God's word."

ELEANOR OF AQUITAINE

"My bold new spouse has sights on England's ring.

When you return, he will be their true king.

He rules by dowry from Narbo to here.

The French monk king lost all and now must fear."

BOETHIUS

"I seek the Frankland the source of my past.

Where public peace presses the die as cast.

Free land where there is no hurt serf or slave.

Leaders who may rule must be fair and brave."

HENRY OF ANJOU - COUNT OF NORMANDY

"The land you seek rests only in your mind.

Many counts and courts are all you will find.

The Breton Forest is empty they say.

Seek the Norman abbey Le Bec this day."

Eleanor of Aquitaine Visits Boethius at the Abbey Le Bec in Normandy Bringing Diana to Be a New Student – 1173 CE

ELEANOR-QUEEN OF ENGLAND, AQUITAINE, ANJOU, NORMANDY AND POITIERS

"Le Bec has been your home for twenty years.

You have known scholastic toil and fears.

I kept the coffers full so you could teach.

And be here to face her wit in the breach?"

BOETHIUS

"You have been bold and direct your whole life.

Your gold, though, may not be worth this new strife.

We do not copy words from an old text.

I will ask questions to puzzle her next."

DIANA

"There is no strict test you may want to ask.

That will provide an unsolvable task.

I do not come as an empty blank slate.

I seek wisdom before it is too late."

ELEANOR - QUEEN OF ENGLAND, AQUITAINE, ANJOU, NORMANDY AND POITIERS

"I know power and how to make it last.

It must feel the future's ties with the past.

Teaching fires this abbey's flame and fame.

She may be the wild horse you cannot tame."

BOETHIUS

"We seek not to chain, but open, her mind.

Her spark is a trait that is hard to find.

I welcome a challenge to start a quest.

Where reason and faith work together best."

Boethius and Diana Engage the Socratic Method at the Abbey Le Bec – 1176 CE

DIANA

"You ask me if we can know God at all.

Such a trick question even for this hall.

We cannot know that which we cannot see.

We cannot propose what never can be."

BOETHIUS

"But surmise a thesis that we may test.

There are perfect shades to act for our best.

God is the one shade better than the rest?

Then, God exists to act on our behest."

DIANA

"You corrupt Anselm and fail as he did.

Your fatal flaw is not easily hid.

You assume God exists to prove it so.

So the answer I say has to be no."

BOETHIUS

"You trust Euclid's logic to be correct.

He has such elegant true proofs to erect.

Yet, he starts with a point he cannot prove.

Even if the rest falls into a set grove."

DIANA

"I see parallel lines without a proof.

They are real and not abstract names aloof.

They predict proven points unlike some wraith.

Logic tells me to accept it on faith."

BOETHIUS

"What is the link between faith and reason?

Is it set or does it change by season?

I believe in God and that explains the rest.

My reason finds faith to solve this true test."

DIANA

"My reason tells me that it is best to look.

Real means more than loose lines found in the Book.

That which exists, then also may not.

My logic cuts through this Gordian knot."

BOETHIUS

"What if it is an accident you see?

And substance is wholly apart ad free?

Does what you see then define what is real?

Or, is truth then just what you want to feel?"

DIANA

"I start with doubt to set logic's own course.

That leads to more questions, but no remorse.

Reason follows to explain what I know.

Leaving me with seeds to nurture and grow."

BOETHIUS

"God set what you seek to observe in place.

He spun the primary compass in space.

His fruits come second, but just as He sought.

Your points denying him have come to naught."

DIANA

"Doubt with joy is the true method of choice.

Our debates are raw so we can rejoice.

You gave me a great gift for these two years.

Yet, I must move on to assuage my fears."

BOETHIUS

"What fears could you have with your nimble mind?

Your skill and insight define their own kind.

Where did you learn well before you came here?

I am not worthy to test you I fear!"

DIANA

"I speak Arabic, French and Occitan.

I pursue Latin, Greek and Corsican."

Mother sent me to Toledo to read.

Ermengard knew my caught mind would be freed."

BOETHIUS

"Am I your father from that fateful night?

Your mother gave birth to a star so bright!

I owe you so much for me not being there.

Now I know I must show you how I care."

DIANA

"The Pope calls you to return to your isle.

Take me too so I can learn how to smile.

I will let nature teach me how to know.

Reason will tender idea seeds to grow."

Boethius and Diana Return to the Springs and Meet King Henry II and Queen Eleanor – 1176 CE

HENRY – KING OF ENGLAND, AQUITAINE, ANJOU, NORMANDY AND POITIERS

"She said next time we met I would be king.

My queen's wit let me take the golden ring.

I rule England by the sprig of the broom.

All because I am Eleanor's young groom."

BOETHIUS

"The Anjou shield shines from Bordeaux to Brest.

Chinon serves you solace above the rest.

Other wry French counts seek to seize a town.

Western France now settles under your crown."

DIANA

"William of Conches taught you how to think.

Reason keeps you from the edge of the brink.

Your wife's gift to me makes my measure whole.

My father and logic animate my soul"

ELEANOR – QUEEN OF ENGLAND, AQUITAINE, ANJOU,| NORMANDY AND POITIERS

"You are Ermengarde's daughter just as well.

You too will lead smartly as time will tell.

Women are power despite their known role.

Hubris and henna will exact their toll."

HENRY – KING OF ENGLAND, AQUITAINE, ANJOU, NORMANDY AND POITIERS

"It is time now not to talk, but to drink.

My dear young child let the springs help you think.

It is a long journey to your home soil.

Your wit will overcome any pain or toil."

Boethius and Laertes, the Newly Appointed Pisan Bishop of Aleria, Observe Diana When They are Approached by Paolo Beyond the Port of Aleria – 1178 CE

BOETHIUS - AID TO THE BISHOP OF ALERIA

"My daughter tests to find a better way.

The people greatly benefit each new day.

Pisa's gold supports her measures to build.

She extends the insight of the mason's guild."

LAERTES - BISHOP OF ALERIA

"I do not know why she marks the high tide.

Does she seek answers or to build her pride?

We need someone to watch each step she takes.

Why does she care why of how each wave breaks?"

PAOLO

"I will undertake the goal that you ask.

That will not be such a hard, daunting task.

I will spy strictly with a keen hawk's eye.

We will know when she may laugh, cringe or cry."

BOETHIUS - AID TO THE BISHOP OF ALERIA

"Abelard sought the same private affair.

He soon lost a lot more than his long hair.

Keep strong your honor and oath that you made.

Lust is no real excuse for them to fade."

LAERTES - BISHOP OF ALERIA

"How will her actions build a better road?

Or, relieve the oxen from their great load?

Report to me all the facts you may see.

Better stones and churches will set us free."

Paolo Observes and Approaches Diana Outside the Port of Aleria Where She is Conducting Tidal Modes Experiments – 1178 CE

PAOLO

"Women have long charted a bold new dream.

Finding in opaque mud a shining seam.

Sica, Deb and Stella taught us to see.

Leading a vanguard that kept us all free."

DIANA

"You caw like a bird lost in a deep fright.

What can I do to keep you from my sight?

I have work to do alone if I might.

I loathe idle eyes lusting for the night."

PAOLO

"I can assist you if you would just ask.

I will improve like wine in an oak cask.

I am like a hoe that clears the fine soil.

I welcome the hardest day's stress and toil."

DIANA

"You want to know whether my breasts are firm.

And how soft are my thighs on a cold berm.

Your ploy is as old as it is now lost.

You will never have my hand at any cost."

PAOLO

"Come to my village where I cannot hide.

Where freedom fosters honor and not pride.

If I have a false faith, then leave me there.

You can abandon me without any care."

Diana Joins Paolo in the Village of Meria Founded by Cor and Sica – 1147 CE

DIANA

"You live where Cor and Sica first did land.

You share their soul when you give me your hand.

Our port touches many coats with surprise.

It forgets how much the mountain is wise."

PAOLO

"Our methods are set as they serve us well.

They can improve more as time soon will tell.

Think of all the tests to put to good use.

Map all angles both acute and obtuse."

DIANA

"My mind races as the questions do not stop.

Why use cold stone terraces for each crop?

How do you get water to those in need?

How do all the cattle know when to feed?"

PAOLO

"The days welcome all the questions you ask.

You still cannot ignore your present task.

Do you want me to join you by your side?

Do we return and measure each new tide?"

LA DONNA DELLA SIGNORA

"Ancient wisdom well informs how she acts.

She pursues the long quest for all the facts.

Logic opens her eyes to what can be.

If she looks right in front of her to see."

The Palace of Emir Nasr of the Almohads in Granada – 1180 CE

EMIR NASR

"We are the last Muslim stronghold in Spain.

Allah blesses us with a fruitful reign.

Stagirite logic solves the hardest test.

Almohad culture satisfies the rest."

MANSUR

"Our troops sit idle with no chant to boast.

Christians taunt us to attack any coast.

The Maghreb trades more with the West each day.

We no longer strike fear, pain or dismay."

EMIR NASR

"My harem is bare and needs a new slave.

A woman of rare beauty, yet still brave.

One like Ermengard who could hunt and think.

Whose whimsy leads to the edge of the brink."

MANSUR

"There is a Corsican that meets your needs.

Few can keep up with all the books she reads.

Her face temps even the newest Moon to blush.

And she is near the troops I want to crush."

EMIR NASR

"Approach slow as if you have come to trade.

Catch her like a young fish ready to wade.

We will chart the arc of the stars at night.

The tiles will receive her glare in the light."

Boethius and Paolo Discover that the Moors Have Abducted Diana from her Tidal Zone – 1180 CE

BOETHIUS

"The Moors move with stealth stealing your young wife.

They swept like the dance of a crescent knife.

There is no hair, flesh, or blood to be found.

An orchestrated plan without a sound."

PAOLO

"I should never have left her alone.

What penance must I do now to atone?

She eschewed all help as she often could.

She did not fear strangers much as she should."

BOETHIUS

"The Moors will rue the day they took this prize.

She will provide them an endless surprise.

Her wit excels when all hope seems so lost.

These Muslims will suffer a wholesale cost."

PAOLO

"I must find her quickly and bring her home.

She cannot waste among the tile and dome.

Let us loose my ship and set a sharp sail.

I must rescue her from her nascent jail."

BOETHIUS

"I knew you would not wait too long to go.

Here is water, food, and a tarp to stow.

Head for Marseilles and then old Narbo too.

Next to the Ebro to pay what is due."

Paolo Meanders Under the Sun on the Great Sea – 1180 CE

PAOLO

"The open sea can be hostile and cruel.

The Sun weathers my skin like an old mule.

I must sail alone to chart my own course.

'Tho I wish I were on land with my horse."

PAOLO'S IMAGINARY FRIEND (WHO IS NOT DEB)

"Do you like how the salt cakes on your lip?

The wind is stagnant stalling your small ship.

You went past the potent Provencal port.

My words burden you while your eyes distort."

PAOLO

"There is no time to try to see it all.

My sloth means my spouse could suffer or fall.

My eyes are blind, yet can follow the Sun.

Straight due west until my honor is done."

PAOLO'S IMAGINARY FRIEND (WHO IS NOT DEB)

"Leather cords dry binding your hands and mast.

Thirst kills any future, present or past.

The waves laugh against the weight of the wood.

As your boat and mind circles as it could."

CLAUDE - CAPTAIN OF A SHIP HEADING FROM NARBO

"Bring water and food for this sinking boat.

Can we help keep it steady and afloat?

Our intrepid Corsican should not die.

Let him finish his trip or at least try."

PAOLO

"Are you Moors trying to end my firm quest?

I am near dead not ready for a test.

You are not Deb or an Ibex that talks.

Is this a dream or a specter that walks?"

CLAUDE - CAPTAIN OF A SHIP HEADING FROM NARBO

"We thought you were a mirage at first sight.

Or a dead man left after a long fight.

We sail from Narbo to trade with the South.

Why are you alone sailing at Death's mouth?"

PAOLO

"The Moors took my wife and I want her back.

I am alone, but I still can attack.

Passion pulses as fuel rather than food.

My armor is just worn out planks of wood."

CLAUDE - CAPTAIN OF A SHIP HEADING FROM NARBO

"We have all the food and water you need.

Tribute to an errant knight's gallant deed.

Sailing too close will soon alert the Moor.

We will drop you off at night on the shore."

PAOLO

"I know I make a fraught solo crusade.

To many it may seem like a charade.

My love and future heirs owe you our fate.

I know now that I will not be too late."

Two Moorish Sentinels, Mohammed and Radio, Walk a Deserted Beach Shore – 1180 CE

MOHAMMED

"What did we do wrong to stand watch each night?

This stretch of bare beach is barren and blight.

Boredom blocks even the stellar light bright.

A moist miasma hovers to mute the light."

RADIO

"Wait, is that body awash on this beach?

Is there excitement within our close reach?

He looks dead, but with a note on his chest.

Should we look or seek some help from the rest?"

MOHAMMED

"The note is in Arabic of some kind.

The Franks do not write our words well I find.

He is a Christian soul taken when young.

Made a eunuch who also lost his tongue."

RADIO

"He returns to us now for his own geste.

Take him to the harem for the true test.

If he died, those women will bring him back.

They will devour him like a wolf pack."

MOHAMMED

"My new friend, you will thank us for this gift.

We will help heal your current empty rift.

The emir has three wives named after Zeus' loves.

And a Corsican gem that wears no gloves."

**Mohammed and Radio Bring Paolo Into the Harem of Emir Nasr in Granada
Where They Meet Leda, Europa and Metis – 1180 CE**

LEDA

"Get out quick you two and let us all be.

Unless, you both have come to set us free.

There is nothing here you can feel or see.

My blade strikes faster than an angry bee."

RADIO

"I see the favors of my grasp and gaze.

Your maze of legs is a ripe field to graze.

But, we bring a present for you to adore.

A young handsome eunuch left on the shore."

EUROPA

"Those two are gone so what is your own tale?

You are no eunuch and can speak as well.

You are the lost son of a forthright race.

Your strong soul may seek solace in this place."

PAOLO

"My wife was taken as a new slave wife.

I must rescue her to complete my life.

She is Diana who owns my hurt heart.

Time presses that it is my time to start."

METIS

"He calls her Calliste just like your isle.

The emir lost to her quick wit and wile.

She pinpoints her curt questions just to vex.

Answers he must know if they are to have sex."

Calliste (Diana) Debates the Emir Nasr in his Chambers – 1180 CE

EMIR NASR

"The tiles' colors frame your beauty so pure.

Your silhouette entices and your locks lure.

Yet, you reject scents, oil and rouge to wear.

Do these Eastern gifts not show that I care?"

CALLISTE (DIANA)

"Do you lust for me or what I might be?

Sheer damask show all that there is to see.

My breasts hold henna verse from Roland's Song.

You must first repent for this Muslim wrong!"

EMIR NASR

"A slave does not tell me what I may do.

I will have what I want when all is through!

I cannot undo what the Basques have done.

You may be clever, but you have not won."

CALLISTE (DIANA)

"Your wits have found an easy place to hide.

The Basques were allies on the Moorish side.

Your clever words fail fast and end up dead.

I will never join you in your down bed."

EMIR NASR

"I tell the oldest stars how bright to shine!

I find their distance between cups of wine.

I master algebra and grammar too.

Yet, you want to dictate what I must do!"

CALLISTE (DIANA)

"You lost Toledo to armies of Rome.

But, you still know the Commentator's tome.

Yet, you profess that Islam is all true.

Allah, not reason, dictates what you do!"

EMIR NASR

"The five stout pillars of my faith are strong.

They enhance reason and cannot be wrong.

Allah bestows logic to be our guide.

This forms a potent unbeatable side."

CALLISTE (DIANA)

"Can there be two pure truths at the same time?

Did logic's shrill death knell just start to chime?

Was the Great Greek right that God is benign?

And reason measures out path and design?"

EMIR NASR

"Allah made us think to know God is right.

He is the cause of the day and the night.

Logic is how we know what we can see.

Reason is faith that makes all of us free."

CALLISTE (DIANA)

"Why must there be a cause for things to be?

Do objects exist that I cannot see?

Should we not pursue more than we are told?

Your answers, as your bed, will remain cold!"

The Guards of Emir Nasr Escort Calliste (Diana) Back to the Harem Not Knowing that Paolo Has Arrived – 1180 CE

CALLISTE (DIANA)

"My hubris may be the death of us all.

My sisters I still defy his beck and call.

He is angry, but wait do my eyes lie?

Paolo arrives so we will not all die!"

PAOLO

"A ship awaits where the river does run.

You three must leave for the warm Gascon Sun.

We are at home in the southern mountains wide.

Her wits know the path to the other side."

LEDA

"How did you know our true Gascon home land?

How can you make such an offer so grand?

You give us your only chance to be free.

You have chosen to die to save us three!"

EUROPA

"Your hubris may kill you both side by side.

We will all have short, steady horses to ride.

Gather the least baggage that you may need.

Let us groom the steads with water and feed."

METIS

"You embrace pure reason over any prayer.

But, may God guide you on a path so fair.

We Gascon women prepare for the fight.

No one will deter our flight this good night."

In the Chambers of Emir Nasr – 1180 CE

EMIR NASR

"Bring me Metis for I did not sleep well.

I must now break Calliste's scornful spell.

I am he who controls all Muslim Spain.

This is no taifa that changes with the rain."

MOHAMMED

"My prince, your four main wives are not in sight.

They seem to have left in the dark deep night.

One brave man led them like old Moses might.

They avoided us guards as well as a fight."

RADIO

"There was a dead man we brought from the shore.

This silent eunuch we left on their floor.

He cannot be found and is missing too.

It seems that Death itself seeks to mock you."

EMIR NASR

"I have twenty thousand men at my call.

And one man steals my wives from my own hall!

I command Mansur to raze their home isle.

We will rebuild it with Moorish blue tile."

MANSUR

"I will find Calliste and bring her back.

They will break from the weight of my attack.

Greek fire will fall like rain in the Spring.

She will soon grovel from the pain I bring."

Mansur and the Moorish Forces Land North of Propriano – 1180 CE

IBN AL S'ALLAH

"She will not be easy to find this time.

They deploy to protect one so sublime.

A direct attack draws out the Pisan fleet.

That is not a marine host we can beat."

MANSUR

"We approach from the west without delay.

We will burn each village along the way.

We will destroy all crops, vines, goats and sheep.

We will take all the slaves we want to keep."

IBN AL S'ALLAH

"The old Vandal troops tried the same approach.

They received a rote ritual reproach

No land was taken, but most men were dead.

Rivers ran fast with Vandal blood so red."

MANSUR

"Our quick troops will win where the Vandals lost.

Our speed will foreclose a similar cost.

Land on the west coast where there is no town.

Let the fire and the ash start to rain down."

IBN AL S'ALLAH

"Ten thousand brave men have hit the rock beach.

Archers and shock troops enter the stone breach.

Lithic paths narrow forcing one straight line.

Eyes watch from dual open stands of pine."

Pascal Paul Piazza

The Moors are Depleted in the Trek from North of Propriano to Outside the Port of Aleria in the Rock Spine of Corsica – 1181 CE

MANSUR

"We will win says the entrails of the birds.

They will pay with pain for her scornful words.

In weeks the port's solid defense will crash.

She will return in chains and cheeks of ash."

IBN AL S'ALLAH

"Our fleet has left to meet us when we win.

But, we file like cows sent to a death pen.

Fire fails to ignite the walls of cold stone.

Our arrows fall back on our heads alone."

MANSUR

"We have beaten the strongest Western knight.

Our men have never withdrawn from a fight.

They are peasants who will run at first sight.

Let our fires brighten their way at night."

IBN AL S'ALLAH

"We face sheer siege walls with no wooden tower.

We cannot move and stall without power.

They block exits and hurl stones from on high.

More than nine-tenths of our best men will die."

MANSUR

"Varus and the Vandals went into this wrath.

Our men should have sought a different path.

Yet, with our remaining troops we will win.

Let the fight for Calliste now begin."

Like Cleopatra Presented to Julius Caesar After Caesar's Victory in Egypt, Emir Nasr is Presented with a Rolled Up Rug After a Brutal Battle Outside the Port of Aleria Where Nine Hundred and Ninety Nine Moors and Eight Hundred Corsicans Died – 1181 CE

RACHMAN, ADMIRAL OF THE ALMOHAD FLEET

"We return from the trip to her rock isle.

Both sides fought long losing both blood and bile.

The piles of dead made columns for prayer.

This rug carries the gifts garnered there!"

EMIR NASR

"Does Calliste lay prone in this new rug?

Like Cleopatra will she be my new drug?

She will succumb to my wit and power.

As she ages slow like a wilted flower."

Rachman, Admiral of the Almohad Fleet

"No, she lives to know and taunt on her own.

While respect for the fallen sides has grown.

Neither brave side withdrew after two days.

Pillage and death overcame their peaceful ways."

EMIR NASR

"How could ten thousand men come to this end.

Is weakness the message we now will send?

Why did you fail to deploy all your men?

You have fresher troops that could help them win!"

RACHMAN, ADMIRAL OF THE ALMOHAD FLEET

"Our ships found the killing field far too late.

We found this message for you at the gate.

Find Mansur and Abdul's heads on a pike.

They did your bidding, but not as you like!"

BOOK TWENTY-ONE

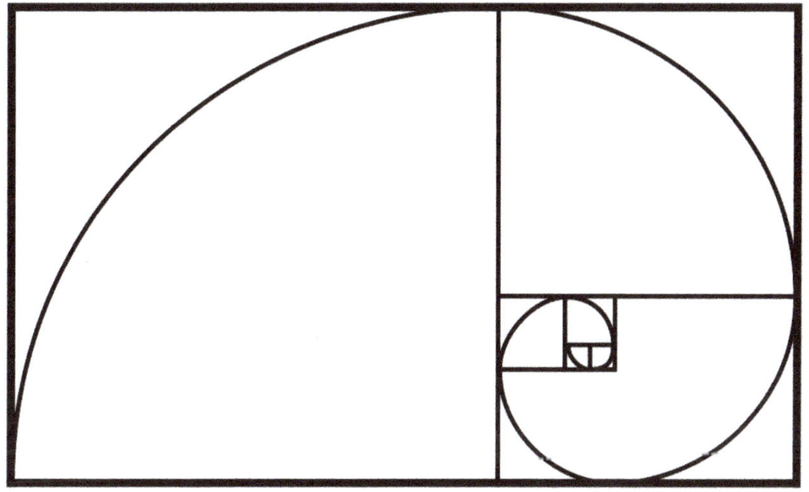

The Medieval Quintet At the Crossroads: Corsica to Cyprus and Genoa's Presence Enlarges – 1181-1195 CE

TASH

"Does the past test how well we live today?

Is it a pithy path showing the way?

Yes, even if we see the past as new.

Our feet will retrace steps both false and true."

PATTI

"Eleanor arrives with a deed to ask.

She invests Diana with a simple task.

Will she mentor Richard's young bride to be?

Will she teach her what a new queen should see?"

BERNADETTE

"Nature gave Diana lessons to teach.

Shortly success was well within her reach.

Storms though cast them captive off Cyprus' coast.

Subject to a rogue Greek emperor's boast."

MARY

"Richard broke off his quest for Acre's walls.

He would save his bride while Cyprus falls.

Templar troops gave Richard the martial edge.

They took Anna to a searcher's steep ledge."

CHARLOTTE

"Back home, Genoa found some land to take.

A foothold to watch the Pisan peace break.

Green eyes saw power, land and flesh to lust.

But, raw force falls to a husband's pure trust."

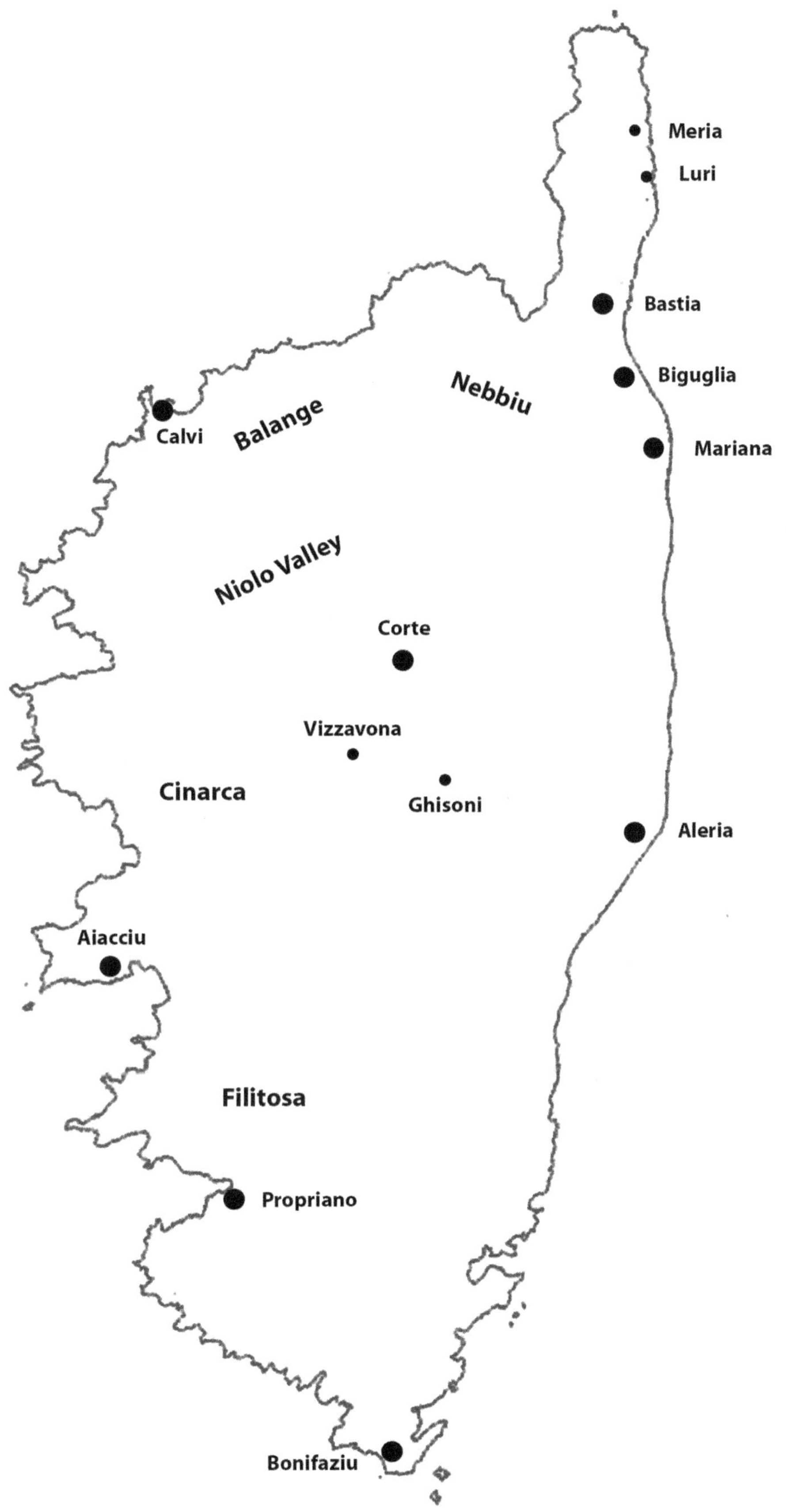

Meria
Luri
Bastia
Biguglia
Nebbiu
Mariana
Calvi
Balange
Niolo Valley
Corte
Vizzavona
Cinarca
Ghisoni
Aleria
Aiacciu
Filitosa
Propriano
Bonifaziu

Biguglia

Gerard of Lorraine Sails Through the Southern Straits of Bonifaziu to Disembark at Aleria to Travel North to Biguglia with a Final Destination in Meria in the Cap Corse – 1180 CE

GERARD OF LORRAINE

"We tack with the timbre of time so clear.

Lorraine lags behind, as my goal draws near.

We had to miss Bonifaziu's shore.

Where Pisa fights pirates in pursuit of war."

JANUS, CAPTAIN OF THE COMMISSIONED SHIP

"Do not focus on the southwest coast's fire.

You search for a place and goal much higher.

An assembly decides how best to rule.

An academy guides each local school."

GERARD OF LORRAINE

"We soon dock in Aleria's peaceful port.

It no longer needs to defend its port.

The Moors I hear head away from this place.

My kin Ursu sought solace in this space."

JANUS, CAPTAIN OF THE COMMISSIONED SHIP

"Biguglia is next by mountain road.

Your fears will be your only burden or load.

Pisa's hub and lagoon will tempt your mind.

But, Meria holds the peace you must find."

GERARD OF LORRAINE

"I disembark to begin my sole quest.

I still do not know which next step is best.

There must be a sign even I can see.

I just need to set my worried mind free."

Anna Cannot be Bothered by Gerard of Lorraine as His Ship Unloads its Passengers and Goods in the Port of Aleria – 1180 CE

ANNA

"I welcome you now, but you are in my way.

I must offload goods from your ship today.

If you care to help, there is room to stay.

And a church nearby if you seek to pray."

GERARD OF LORRAINE

"How can you dismiss me with just a glance?

I am proficient with sword and lance.

I could be wanted in most of France.

I may have drugs to put you in a trance."

ANNA

"Your double cross tells me that you are lost.

But, if you harm us, you will pay the cost.

The school runs new tests as my present task.

I am not here for all the questions you ask."

GERARD OF LORRAINE

"Then, I should enroll as I start my quest.

Though, I may be different than the rest.

I come to find that which may not exist.

A cynic's life that just seeks to subsist."

ANNA

"A cynic does not trust what the eyes see.

Go observe how the maquis remains free.

Find the debt each village elder pays.

Meet me at the lagoon in fourteen days."

Gerard of Lorraine Returns After Fourteen Days in the Mountain Villages West of Biguglia to Meet Anna Who is Conducting Tests on the Lagoon in Biguglia

GERARD OF LORRAINE

"Conflict defines the balance of life.

The village is calm, yet deals with great strife.

Robust threats abound that should cause despair.

Yet, the resilient maquis remains there."

ANNA

"We have our way that is forthright and fair.

We keep strict to ourselves, but we still care.

The counts want castles and estates to rule.

We have communes, debates, and my true school."

GERARD OF LORAINE

"The commune's debate was strident and long.

Feelings were hot and the passion was strong.

Yet, even the smallest valley was heard.

Freedom followed each and every word."

ANNA

"A smile is not the only way to show fear.

Joy masks the grievance that is always near.

Have you now found what you are looking for?

I believe you lack the key for fate's door."

GERARD OF LORRAINE

"Meria is where I must seek to go.

The coast road is good, but my steps are slow.

I still choose to digest all that I see.

It is in this trip that I will be free."

Gerard of Lorraine Encounters Sogno, a Masero, in Meria

SOGNO, A MASERO

"You are not from this village or our clan.
You walk with a purpose, but have no plan.
You travel on ground where all eyes can see.
I travel in dreams where time remains free."

GERARD OF LORRAINE

"Long ago, Basina's son came this way.
Seeking such solace and a space to stay.
I trace those steps to fulfill my soul's will.
But, I still need the passion, path and skill."

SOGNO, A MASERO

"You know this is a dream where you must die?
Yet, you persist to live not knowing why?
Ursu's clan will meet you with blindless faith.
I am just a simple and senseless wraith."

GERARD OF LORRAINE

"I do not know how you speak of my loss.
The Roberts are dead 'tho they wore the Cross.
Anjou took their land by strokes of a blade.
Son fights father to show how strength is made."

SOGNO, A MASERO

"Ursu once was lost, but then he was found.
His chains were cut leaving his mind unbound.
He found his soul where it always had been.
His freedom came from his debt to his kin."

Gerard of Lorraine Arrives in the Academy of Aleria Founded by Diana and her Principal Teachers and Former Students, Anna and Hector, After a Two-Week Trip to Meria in the Cap Corse

GERARD OF LORRAINE

"I learned that my duty is not a place.

It does not care what steps I may re-trace.

I saw now what before I could not see.

A dream foretold of my soon death to be."

DIANA

"What you observe sparks the flame of reason.

A light that burns bright for any season.

Tell us now what you saw in your true quest.

What supplied answers to your vexing test."

GERARD OF LORRAINE

"The Pisan peace courses through the paths of stone.

Each village shares bonds yet still is alone.

The commune thrives even while threats abound.

Fairness, honor, hope and justness resound."

DIANA

"Trust what your eyes reveal what you have found.

But, know the earth often shifts below ground.

Duty does not change, but foes often do.

Be vigilant to forces both old and new."

GERARD OF LORRAINE

"Genoa's ships search the south when they can.

They seek to destroy Pisa's central plan.

Pisa ousts these "pirates" to restore peace.

This island stays an intact golden fleece."

Diana Continues Anna's Training in the Academy in Aleria

DIANA

"Do you understand Euclid's Golden Mean?

How can it be both seen and yet unseen?

Does reason tempt us to play its own game?

Does anything exist without its own name?"

ANNA

"Should I care what may or may not exist?

When concrete and stone survive and persist?

Thoughts only count on paper in my hand.

The mason's mind constructs designs so grand."

DIANA

"You search for the part, but not for the whole.

You ignore the conch for a single pole.

Its spiral is endless, yet still concrete.

Its curves mark truth both abstract and discrete."

ANNA

"Nature may guide us if we choose to look.

But our compass is found in a real book.

We will solve the new tasks before us now.

Euclid's text, not a shell, will show us how."

DIANA

"The ancient scrolls began in Euclid's mind.

Words follow sight in both substance and kind.

Method is the compass tied with the level.

One must imagine to yield a true bevel."

Hector and a Troop Perform the Spiral Procession of the Granitula Outside Aleria While the Fleet of Queen Eleanor of Aquitaine and Berengaria of Navarre (Fiancée of King Richard the Lionheart) Approach – 1181 CE

ANNA

"White cloaks delimit the set outside line.

Blue cloaks form shrinking inside spirals fine.

Then reverse up the spirals to the start.

The math I know, but not the music part."

POLYPHONIC SINGING[1]

"U mo paese hè u mo core.

Hè u polzudi e rocce fredde.

Starraghja ancu s'e partu prestu.

U grand delore nè u mo fruttu."[2]

DIANA

"They sing: Their village animates their heart.

It is the blood pulse that makes cold rocks start.

They will stay even if they must leave soon.

Great pain is their fruit under the bright moon."

ANNA

"They are a discrete abstract in one time,

Their path shrinks in shape to find the Great Prime.

They are playful, yet stern in their soul chant.

Satire cackles in geste with a cold rant."

DIANA

"They make the Granitula and sing.

They shrink the spiral with each new ring.

Curves mark death for ever ending life.

Honor the Virgin and Good Friday's strife."

---

1   Unique form of Corsican a *cappella* singing.
2   My village is my heart. It is the pulse of the cold rocks. I will stay even I leave soon. Great pain is my fruit.

ELEANOR, DOWAGER QUEEN OF ENGLAND

"Yet, no such holy day fete should be seen.

They mock the Three Lions' flag and its queen.

They know we come wearing the new white cross.

To invite you to join a crusading loss."

DIANA

"I am glad that you have not lost your wit.

I feared you now were a horse with a bit.

Look and what we and Ermengard would do.

Life will spin like a top when we are through."

ELEANOR, DOWAGER QUEEN OF ENGLAND

"That focus is why I am here this day.

Moors are no match for the foe I must slay.

I bring Richard his new young wife to be.

She lacks guile and tact, but her mind is free."

DIANA

"I have no counsel to help her in bed.

I work all of the time and am not well fed.

You mastered kings of both England and France.

Your wit informs her to compose a trance."

GODFREY

"Richard awaits in cold Sicilian halls.

He wants to join Phillip at Acre's walls.

We must move now with little time to lose.

You need to act now the path that you choose."

ELEANOR, DOWAGER QUEEN OF ENGLAND

"Her hand to Richard keeps my realm secure.

Her steadfast true traits are not her sole lure.

She thinks reason will assuage royal fights.

She needs your guidance to focus her sights."

DIANA

"Do I have time to earn her nascent trust?

She is not some debased metal with rust.

It is method that commands us to know.

And not just planting seeds in rows to sow."

ELEANOR, DOWAGER QUEEN OF ENGLAND

"Phillip and Richard head to Acre's gate.

We are behind with little time to wait.

You two must find Joan, Sicily's lost queen.

Then, East to restore Outremer's lost gleam."

DIANA

"That is not likely to be a smooth path.

We intersect royal fits and war's wrath.

I must bring Hector and Anna with me.

Then, we will soon see that what we can see."

ELEANOR, DOWAGER QUEEN OF ENGLAND

"You and I have very much to review.

Hattin's loss means all we know is askew.

Richard and Phillip ally until they fight.

Keep both Anjou and Paris in your sight."

Diana and Berengaria Have a Conversation on the Deck of the Ship Above the Waves and the Ubiquitous Spiral Shells – 1191 CE

BERENGARIA, FIANCÉE OF KING RICHARD THE LIONHEART

"It is two days to Messina's stone shores.

Many less days you had to teach the Moors.

You were at Le Bec for more than a year.

Is there time to overcome my doubts and fears."

DIANA

"My time with the Moors was as a captive.

Le Bec blurs while my mind is restive.

Watch the waves become opaque and then clear.

You will soon lose your doubt or fictive fear."

BERENGARIA, FIANCÉE OF KING RICHARD THE LIONHEART

"I can see why eyes are special for you.

Spiral shells shelter in sand grains too.

Nature watches me just like Richard's spies.

They see the truth and cannot create lies."

DIANA

"They are St. Lucy's eyes seeking true Light.

Even though she sought to blind her own sight.

To see is a gift that very few know.

Light makes shadows in the picture to show."

BERENGARIA, FIANCÉE OF KING RICHARD THE LIONHEART

"I also see spirals in the dark night sky.

Joining dances and shells to dare to ask why.

Richard is a comet with his own light.

Is that why I can see stars in the night?"

The Party Docks at Naples Where it Queen Joan Meets Them

DIANA

"You are not here to bask in Richard's glow.

You seek the tact and wit wisdom must know.

You set the course that the comet may take.

And command real results that are not fake."

MALLORY, CAPTAIN OF THE KING'S GUARD

"The King bids that you dock in Naples' Bay.

Queen Joan will meet you as you make your way.

You have too many ships for other shores.

The King has just left to fight Acre's Moors."

JOAN, DOWAGER QUEEN OF SICILY

"My brother fears most that Acre soon falls.

Phillip already fights outside its walls.

He did restore our name and honor here.

That his duty is in the East in clear."

ELEANOR, DOWAGER QUEEN OF ENGLAND

"You trust your brother like none I have seen.

I hope he feels the same for his new queen.

She must go East as I once did before.

She will build his stature in this just war."

BERENGARIA, FIANCÉE OF KING RICHARD THE LIONHEART

"Let us be pilgrims and journey now East.

My weeding can join sweet victory's feast.

Eleanor returns home to keep the peace.

We are like heroes in search of our fleece."

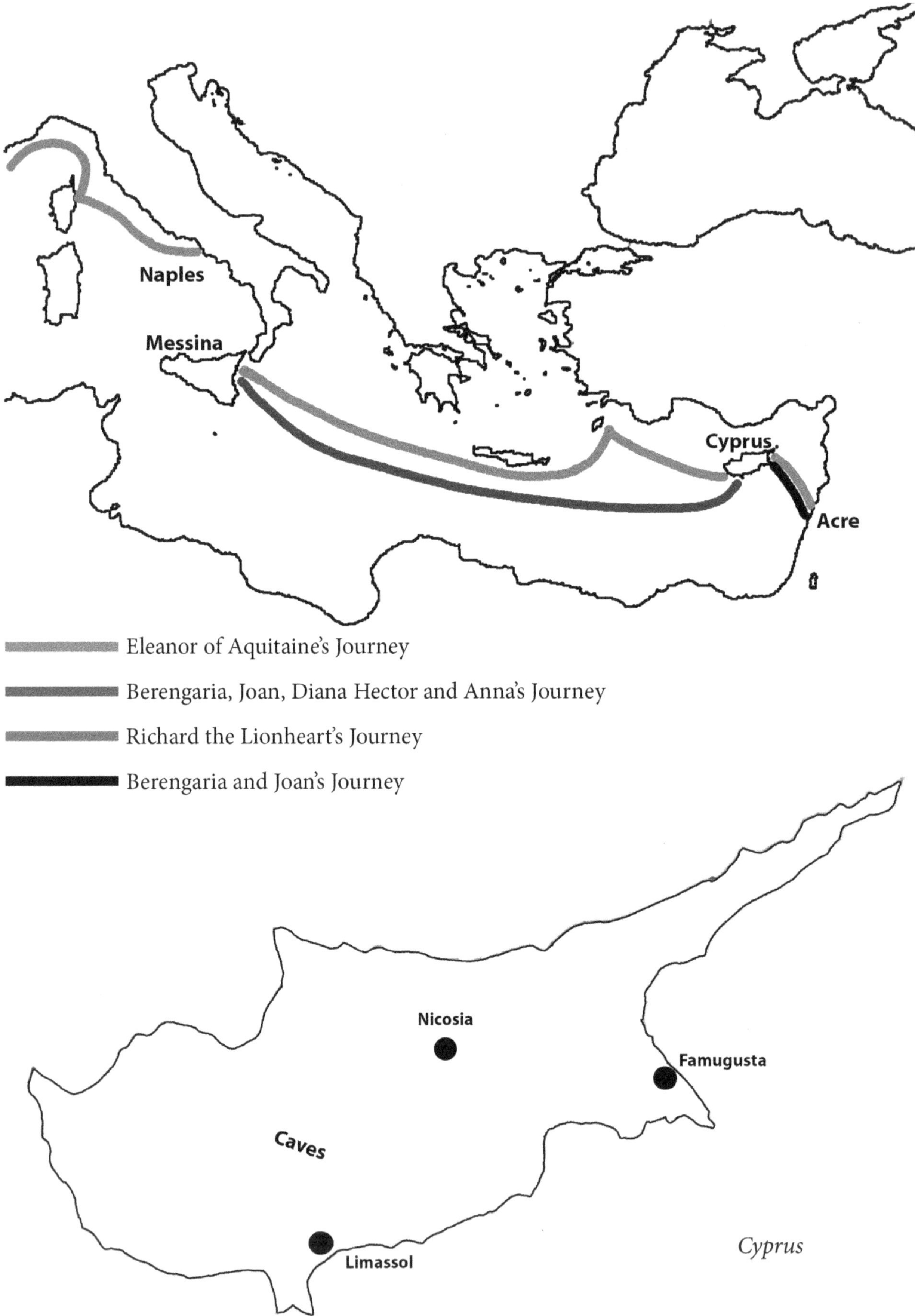

Naples
Messina
Cyprus
Acre
Eleanor of Aquitaine's Journey
Berengaria, Joan, Diana Hector and Anna's Journey
Richard the Lionheart's Journey
Berengaria and Joan's Journey
Nicosia
Famugusta
Caves
Limassol
Cyprus

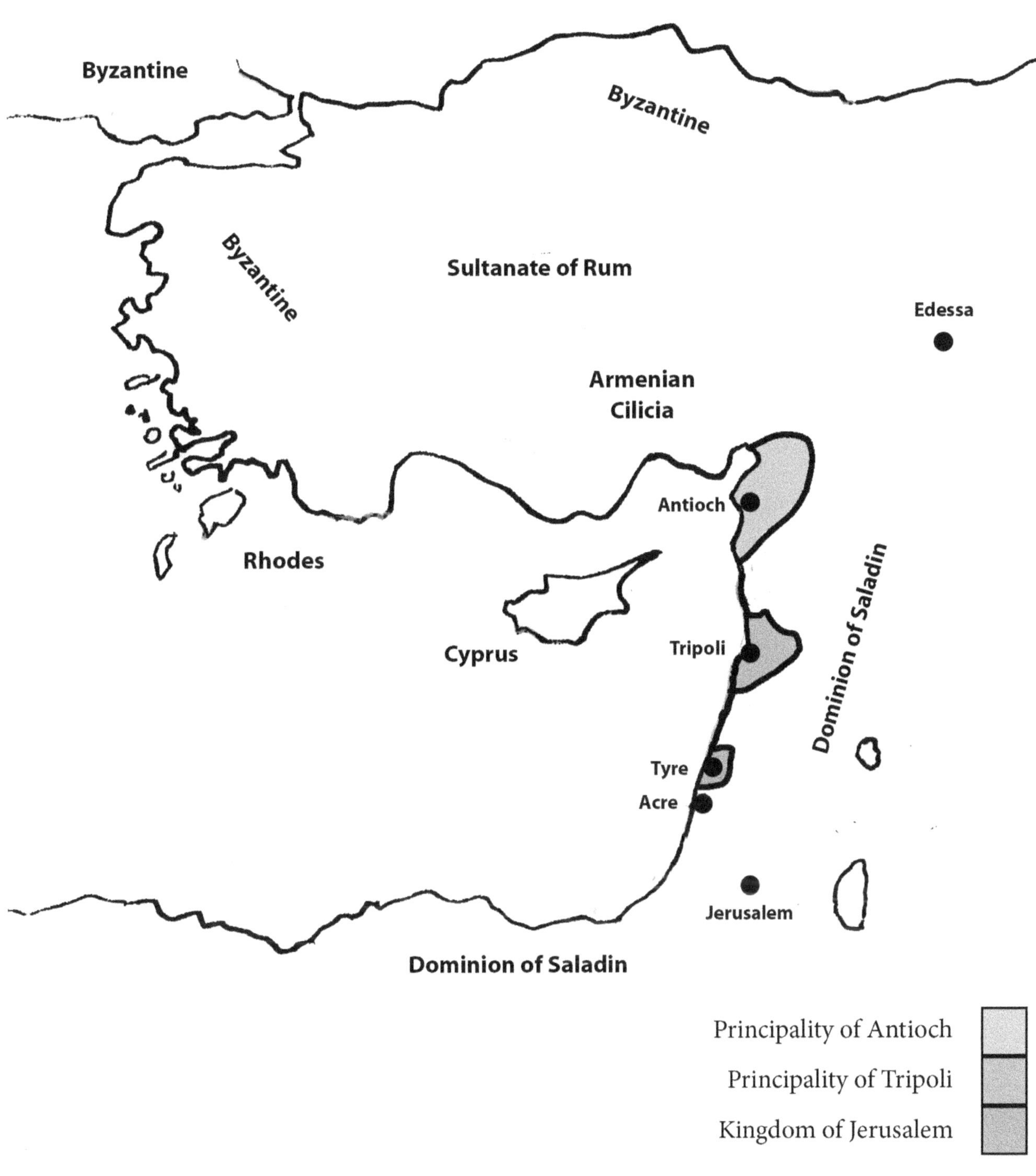

Outremer at the Beginning of the Third Crusade – 1191 CE

Diana and Berengaria Continue the Teaching as the Ships Near the Island of Cyprus – 1191 CE

BERENGARIA, FIANCÉE OF KING RICHARD THE LIONHEART

"Why do we paint our image on each star.

Is the dark sky just black-slip on a jar?

Does that make Venus greet us each new morn?

Do we seek control or just our own scorn?"

DIANA

"We project what we see so we can know.

Orion's hunt make the fast night sky slow.

Yet, ships must track currents not some old name.

To ignore what occurs just leads to blame."

MALLORY, CAPTAIN OF THE KING'S GUARD

"Quickly, go inside before the gale strikes.

Waves soon pierce the wood hull like precise pikes.

We do not want to find out if you float.

Pray the cooper made good joints for this boat."

JOAN, DOWAGER QUEEN OF SICILY

"This is but a soft drizzle of cold rain.

I have felt the sharp dagger of real pain.

We are captives within a wooden womb.

We shall walk as pilgrims before His Tomb."

BERENGARIA, FIANCÉE OF KING RICHARD THE LIONHEART

"We may never reach Richard or his quest.

He will never see me at my true best.

We are strong together in this cold night.

This is but a test of our common might."

Joan, Berengaria, Diana, Anna, and Hector Wait Out the Storm in Hammocks Designed by Anna

HECTOR

"Our hammocks suspend still in silent space.

We are immune from the storm's raging pace.

Boarded windows block the light and each star.

The tempest could be near or could be far."

ANNA

"This is like when I fell in a cave's hole.

Stuck and static and cold to my lost soul.

Not knowing hurt more than a course spear's point.

Time's laugh pierces my marrow between each joint."

BERENGARIA, FIANCÉE OF KING RICHARD THE LIONHEART

"Are we a chrysalis in a cocoon?

Waiting to emerge in some new lagoon?

Thunder teases as time pulses with our fear.

There is small hope that land soon will appear."

JOAN, DOWAGER QUEEN OF SICILY

"I have been a hostage for my own good.

Less than twelve, I wed like a daughter should.

Then, I lost power along with my spouse.

Later, I was captive in my own house."

DIANA

"There is a rage matching Richard's full wrath.

It is this storm guiding your direct path.

Euclid's genius gives us a chance to live.

The rope lets the hammock forget and give."

The Ship Moors Off the Port of Limassol, Cyprus which is Controlled by the Rogue Pretender Byzantine Emperor Isaac Who Sees an Opportunity to Take Royal Hostages to Leverage Relations with the West After Entering an Alliance with the Sultan Saladin – April 28, 1191 CE

MALLORY, CAPTAIN OF THE KING'S GUARD

"Break open the door and release our Queen.

This gale has been the worst I had ever seen.

Yet, you each arise like you have slept well.

You emerge like gods from a mythic tale."

JOAN, DOWAGER QUEEN OF SICILY

"Have we found a dry land of friend or foe?

After the deluge, there should be great woe.

How are our troops and dedicated crew?

The storm only paused the tasks we must do."

MALLORY, CAPTAIN OF THE KING'S GUARD

"We are in Cyprus, a Byzantine land.

Led by Isaac who soothes Saladin's hand.

The troop ship sunk with a few who survive.

They are in cold chains, but they are alive."

JOAN, THE DOWAGER QUEEN OF SICILY

"Raise Richard's flags and announce who we are.

We are pilgrims that have come very far.

By treaty, safe passage now is our right.

We seek Isaac's refuge and not a fight."

MALLORY, CAPTAIN OF THE KING'S GUARD

"Isaac is a rogue allied with the Moors.

Your men now reside behind prison doors.

You know the perfidy such friends can show.

Fealty follows the winds as they may blow."

Isaac Meets with Mansur, Saladin's Cousin, in Limassol – April 28, 1191 CE

MANSUR

"Richard's grand fleet has been broken apart.

He comes to finish what Phillip did start.

His main force delays in Rhodes far from here.

But, strewn ships make a wood bridge far and near."

ISAAC

"You act as if we have already lost.

My defenses disclose that I have spared no cost.

A ship with his flag moors within my grasp.

I will capture once the new peace does lapse."

MANSUR

"You cannot take hostages as you like.

Break the old treaty and Richard must strike.

You are Roman and thus of the same blood.

You cannot survive the consuming flood."

ISAAC

"I do what I want to do and when I will.

There is but one small ship alone and still.

I will extend the palm, but seize the day.

Richard will pledge his fealty and hope to pray."

MANSUR

"Your great hubris, great prince, leads you astray.

I have no more sage words to help you today.

Richard's rage masters misery and fears.

Cyprus will be lost to the West for years."

The Ship Lists Dead in the Port of Limassol – April 29, 1091 CE

MALLORY, CAPTAIN OF THE KING'S GUARD

"We have no more sails, oars, rudder or mast.

We are in stasis in a die now cast.

You exhibit ennui, yet eschew gifts.

Low water and food soon will reveal rifts."

JOAN, DOWAGER QUEEN OF SICILY

"These gifts ask us to embrace golden chains.

Our host marshals troops on his coastal plains.

Diana and I were captives before.

This peace charade hides the onset of war."

BERENGARIA, FIANCÉE OF KING RICHARD THE LIONHEART

"Our men should not have to suffer for me.

I want to see that all our men are free.

Yet, I see how they treat our men onshore.

We have no choice but to prepare for war."

DIANA

"My love found me, as Richard will find you.

But, you need not now be a hostage too.

We can last many more hard and longer days.

We relish our wits, rights, and long free ways."

ANNA

"A single ship comes from the north this day.

We know the honied words they wish to say.

Our wits will remain our buckler and shield.

As one, we shall tempt death before we yield."

Heraclitus, Isaac's General Tries One Last Time for the Ship to Surrender – May, 12, 1191 CE

HERACLITUS

"Isaac is the emperor of all Rome.

Accept our gifts and offer of a home.

Richard is sea-sick, as storms again rise.

His fleet will not survive Nature's surprise."

JOAN, DOWAGER QUEEN OF SICILY

"Your lips move fast, as we are slow to trust.

Your words are like a relic of pure rust.

Your truculent disdain shows you are weak.

You lack the backbone to take what you seek."

HERACLITUS

"You affect a good front with fearless style.

But, you lack your mother's wit, tact and guile.

Will you speak this way when more ships arrive?

Your words will be woeful if you survive!"

HECTOR

"There are more sails than the stone beach has sand.

It is Richard's force that invests the land.

His rage makes a robust tempest seem tame.

Torches makes a bright comet's tail with his fame."

ANNA

"Isaac's troops broke without giving a fight.

Limassol falls before day becomes night.

Our men will have care and the food they need.

This will be the pure end to Isaac's greed."

King Richard the Lionheart Discusses the Administration of Cyprus and Outremer with Guy de Lusignan, Geoffrey de Lusignan, and Gerard, a Templar Master – June 10, 1191 CE

KING RICHARD THE LIONHEART

"In one month, Isaac is in silver chains.

New taxes fill my burse like new Spring rains.

My health though pauses relief of Acre's strife.

It also delays the joys of my new wife."

GUY DE LUSIGNAN

"You took the cross after Hattin's sad wake.

I fought the next four years for your true sake.

We held out for the strength just you could bring.

Now, I too will again be the true king."

GEOFFREY DE LUSIGNAN

"Leave the Templars here to hold your conquest.

Acre remains the grail of your true quest.

Phillip and Conrad get all of the fame.

You must spark the fire of fealty's flame."

GERARD, A TEMPLAR MASTER

"Cyprus is a base we must keep intact.

Let us enter into a solemn pact.

We supply the reconquest the Pope craves

While we search for the gold in Isaac's caves."

KING RICHARD THE LIONHEART

"We delay no more and seek to attack.

The Templars will rule until I come back.

My wife will travel to Acre with me.

She will shine when Jerusalem is free."

Lucca, a Corsican Templar, Rescues Hector at a Bar in Limassol

NICOLE

"You do not wear Lionheart's white cross brand.

I too am a stranger in a strange land.

Let me comfort you in a foreign way.

You will burst with pulsating words to say."

HECTOR

"You are kind, but I choose to be alone.

The cross's riddle weighs heavy like a stone.

Is this just a contest between two kings?

Is this the weight that this pilgrimage brings?

NICOLE

"Let us see who can drink more of these shots.

It is more certain than gambling with lots.

If you win, you will have me and much more.

If I win, your sword will even the score."

LUCCA, A CORSICAN TEMPLAR

"Let the tip of my sword make its true point.

Need I flay your flesh now from joint to joint?

You drink water while he consumes alcohol.

Your vile scam is designed to make him fall."

HECTOR

"Thank you, but she meant no real harm this day.

She was a test of my doubt on display.

My thoughts return home with the truth you show.

What is your home village and who do know?"

LUCCA

"I am from Siscu and the Balba clan.

She tried to trick you as part of her plan.

She would drink water that looks like hard drink.

She would then rob you when you could not think."

ANNA

"Lucca's vow is to help pilgrims in need.

He was just doing his sworn Templar deed.

Not that I was concerned in any way.

She could not stay to hear what you would say."

HECTOR

"But, I gave no sign that I needed help.

There was no fatal fall or a dog's yelp.

Why did he choose to assist me in need?

What prompted him to give a Templar's deed?"

LUCCA, A CORSICAN TEMPLAR

"I share the same true vow that you both share.

We act to do good to show we do care.

We are Corsicans and that is our soul.

I am proud to honor our steadfast role."

ANNA

"He was not near you simply by odd chance.

I know you can get lost in some dull trance.

We are on this island for our true test.

Lucca can guide us to complete our quest."

LUCCA, A CORSICAN TEMPLAR

"The Templars dug beneath the Temple Mound.

They will not tell you the relics they found.

Tunnels connect so they cannot be seen.

Each cave here is a source for gifts to glean."

ANNA

"Isaac did not fight, but he hid his goods.

He used caves just north among the old woods.

We must be like the Templars and explore.

We do not know what the caves have in store."

HECTOR

"Are we pilgrims seeking treasure to find?

Does gold provide the moral tie to bind?

Maybe, we should have set sail for His Land.

We could kill and still find gold in this land!"

LUCCA, A CORSICAN TEMPLAR

"Listen, she seeks the baton of the boar.

Where no pilgrims have sought to search before.

The clues point to the caves up north just found.

This surpasses some relic in the ground."

ANNA

"Cyprus is due west from where it was lost.

Saladin wants this island at all cost.

Celts before sought copper to make bronze spears.

The Celts have not been here for many years."

HECTOR

"Isaac is a Greek and never a Moor.

He may be a mock Roman at his core.

The clues thus do not apply to this place.

This will not change regardless of our pace."

ANNA

"One who allies with a Moor is a Moor.

Isaac allies with Moors to fund his war.

Therefore, Isaac is a mock Moor to me.

Logic tells me we are where we should be."

LUCCA

"Cyprus was sold to the Templar Order.

They will soon secure each cave and border.

You are free to explore before we do.

You should find the baton as you are due."

HECTOR

"I should never doubt her intrepid mind.

Her pure insight makes her one of a kind.

I am sorry if I cast doubt on you.

I just need time to think this bold plan through."

ANNA

"Time will measure whether it stops or flies.

We should be weary when the truth lies.

I enjoy making you think I am mad.

Let us ask if this plan is good or bad."

Anna, However, Does Not Wait and Enters the Caves Alone. Anna Hallucinates and Carries on a Dialogue (of Sorts) with an Imaginary Anna – September 1191 CE

ANNA

"How do I determine which cave to choose?

I must act as there is no time to lose.

The Templars take time to marshal their force.

They must have their picks, tools, scaffolds and horse."

IMAGINARY ANNA

"What did you think about acting alone?

Are you curious or must you atone?

You fell in a cave when you were a child.

Can you overcome new forces strong and wild?"

ANNA

"Where would I hide the baton if I could?

No, rather I must think like Isaac would.

This cave seems to hide from the other eight.

All right, it is time for me to tempt Fate."

IMAGINARY ANNA

"The high walls and roof make our slow heart race.

Our feet slip on loose rocks slowing our pace.

The walls show a touch of a master's hand.

Maybe, we should just return to dry land."

ANNA

"I sense a fake wall that smoke can reveal.

Water or light pass where there is no seal.

There must be a path hidden from my sight.

My candle flickers turning day to night."

IMAGINARY ANNA

"The ceiling is a gracile cobbled vault.

Why is there a blank wall making us halt?

We should let the Templars move this faux wall.

There would be no help if we were to fall."

ANNA

"Can I dislodge the wall with my own mind?

I wish there were a long lever to find.

I must now summon the forces that I need.

I can ignore the cut skin that may bleed."

IMAGINARY ANNA

"An open door does not mean we must look.

That is why I prefer reading a book.

I know that we must apply what we learn.

We will soon have to crawl before we turn."

ANNA

"What lurks ahead makes all my humors spike.

It is like Nature just pierced me with a pike.

The rock is flat 'til only I can slide.

Stuck again, my memory is my guide."

IMAGINARY ANNA

"I need not tell us that we cannot move.

We are stuck helpless in this lithic groove.

We got out before and we will once more.

That seems trite as our muscles are so sore."

Anna Speaks with Daedalus in His Cave

ANNA

"I am stuck in a double-axe form vise.

Its inventor is both careful and wise.

My torso stays put in a balanced groove.

I observe time pass in sync while my arms move."

DAEDALUS

"You are the first one ever to reach here.

Yet, you do not yelp, shriek, cry, or show fear.

You have no eyes of avarice or greed.

I sense that there is something you need."

ANNA

"I want to know how you built this device.

To be sent home now would never suffice.

I also seek the lost baton of the boar.

It will help my people's character soar."

DAEDALUS

"Diana has taught you what you must know.

Intrepid questions are the seeds to sow.

I can let you down without any fear.

You only seek answers, so please come near."

ANNA

"How do you know who my teacher has been?

I must ask too much: who, what, why and when?

I came before the Templars make their way.

Your faux wall will not keep them long at bay."

DAEDALUS

"I am a terrible host while we talk.
You need some food, water and a brief walk.
Let your mind embrace the labyrinth test.
As I explain the key to all the rest."

DAEDALUS

"There once was true symmetry and balance.
Minds, hearts and life were a value valance.
Val, Deb, Merlin and I held wisdom's key.
Elements and traits that kept mortals free."

DAEDALUS

"Val was the clever dichotomy of night.
Deb was cynical prudence found in sight.
Merlin was mystery and the unknown.
I built what could not be built or soon known."

DAEDALUS

"Time and order unwound in stone with grace.
They were abrupt when not in uniform pace.
We each were part of the resulting whole.
We all were the full universal soul."

DAEDALUS

"Val became bored and proposed a new path.
We were blind that it would lead to such wrath.
She said, "Find a host for all your knowledge.
They will be in one place under our pledge.""

DAEDALUS

"I built a temple that was so secure.

There was no true key to lose to lust's lure.

Each day we went in and out at one time.

We kept our oath in a manner sublime."

DAEDALUS

"Val found out that I had put in a back door.

No one else had used it any time before.

In stark moonlight, Val took wisdom's power.

She hid it from us in her own tower."

DAEDALUS

"The Moon arose red and hid the new Sun.

Soon all that was done quickly was undone.

Magma cut through the crust spreading it out.

Chaos broke through time and space seeding doubt."

DAEDALUS

"Val raised an army and seized all the land.

Time and water lost to her fiery brand.

We three fought her with each trick that we knew.

The standing stones shook until we were through."

DAEDALUS

"Val did not know that the hosts were half full.

There was a short time fuse for her to rule.

Deb made her men dolmens and menhirs too.

Signs not to abuse the strength that is true."

DAEDALUS

"The temple fell and its stones used for good.

Our three hosts were refilled as best we could.

They were split up never to be as one.

Culture had to learn from lessons undone."

DAEDALUS

"One went East where the Temple Mound is found.

The Phaistos Disk was laid well underground.

The baton and books went to Deb's own home.

The keys seek the mind while hosts do not roam."

DAEDALUS

"The Templars did find wisdom in their quest.

The disk will be an afterthought at best.

Do like the Templars and search when you can.

Asking questions will be the soul of man."

DAEDALUS

"You will not find the baton where you are.

Since its loss, it has traveled very far.

Search where Zeus's son kneels bright in the dark night.

The faux Moors await ready for a fight."

DAEDALUS

"My tale lasts too long so I now must sleep.

I hope you have found some wisdom to keep.

Your friends must think that you have gone astray.

In fact, you alone have found the true way."

Daedalus Disappears in the Cave While Hector and Lucca Lament in Limassol that They Have Failed Anna and Diana

HECTOR

"How could I let Anna roam off alone?

Her passion was as strong as the cold stone.

But, I thought she would join the Templar quest.

And avoid the pain of a solo test."

LUCCA

"I too thought she would remain at our side.

She would not make the mistakes we had tried.

I was blind to her bold curious soul.

To find the baton is her single goal."

DIANA

"Why do you forget all that I taught you?

She pursued a path she knew was true.

Truth is her companion and her true guide.

She did not need anyone else by her side."

ANNA

"Why do the men look like someone has died.

It is time to return home with the tide.

The baton still rests outside these cave walls.

Cyprus is at peace while Acre soon falls."

DIANA

"We Corsicans have now left our own mark.

We live the proof of wisdom's special spark.

A queen now knows how to guide and rule.

Wit and tact take us back to our own school."

Bonifaziu

Ors Alamanno a Genoese General, Leads a Genoese Force to Invest Bonifaziu Hidden Behind the Steep White Cliffs Overlooking the Straight of Bonifaziu – 1195 CE

ORS ALMANNO, GENOESE COMMANDER

"These steep white cliffs discourage an attack.

Yet, we move forward to take and to sack.

I know a break in these natural walls.

The city will be ours when it soon falls."

AMERIGO, GENOESE CAPTAIN

"Do we besiege the town with naval might?

Ten ships moor ready to bombard tonight.

Or, do we land further along the shore?

And use the land to start our total war?"

ORS ALMANNO, GENOESE COMMANDER

"No, they will open the gates when we ask.

They will invite us to perform our task.

The sentinel city seeks our sole reign.

Then we subdue the free-men of the plain."

AMERIGO, GENOESE CAPTAIN

"They think we are here just for the money.

We want to rule not find wax and honey.

Our troops stand ready to march in order.

Proudly set to extend Genoa's border."

ORS ALMANNO, GENOESE COMMANDER

"Our goal has long been to break Pisa's back.

We get closer as we start this attack.

We will take this key island piece by piece.

'Til Pisa withdraws when it sues for peace."

The Genoese Force First Engages and Then Makes Peace with a Force of Free Men Defending Their Homes Located in the Villages Located on the Plains Near or Outside Bonifaziu – 1195 CE

ANTONIO PIOBETTA, THE CORSICAN LEADER

"You have no choice now but to leave this field.

We will not succumb, pay homage, or yield.

Fight us and lose all that you sought to gain.

Your rule will measure the depths of pure pain."

ORS ALMANNO, GENOESE COMMANDER

"We have an army that dwarfs your small ranks.

You will spill blood filling your rivers' banks.

We kill with modern skill and precision.

Whether death or life is your decision."

ANTONIO PIOBETTA, THE CORSICAN LEADER

"Many Vandals and Moors made your mistake.

Recall the captain's head on a sharp stake.

Pisa could build by leaving us alone.

We gave them gifts with no need to atone."

ORS ALMANNO, GENOESE COMMANDER

"Do you offer us a peace pact this day?

You remain free with just taxes to pay?

We can rule the city at our leisure?

You will have the families you treasure?"

ANTONIO PIOBETTA, THE CORSICAN COMMANDER

"I seal this pact with my word and this horse.

Let rectitude guide us on this new course.

The town can host your Ligurian lust.

But, I warn you if you break this true trust!"

***Ors Almanno and Amerigo Ride Among the Villages, Ors Almanno Accosts Paolo's Wife
Under a Ruler's Rights and Breaks the Trust, Paolo Confronts Ors Almanno,
and Amerigo and Paolo Restore the Peace – 1195 CE***

AMERIGO, GENOESE CAPTAIN

"The crisp air and herbal scent restore health.

I can see why they think this is their wealth.

I have seen the horse the Turks like the best.

Your gift stead excels and supplants the rest."

ORS ALMANNO, GENOESE COMMANDER

"This horse is fine, but whose face glows with dew.

Breasts and thighs entice just like her face too.

I claim my right to each woman I like.

Try to keep up with me while I soon strike."

AMERIGO, GENOESE CAPTAIN

"My horse's gallop is a slow slothful slog.

The dirt impedes me like a doleful bog.

I wait to see what has happened ahead.

Oh God, there is a long pike with his head."

ANTONIO PIOBETTA

"I drew a line no man could ever cross.

The loss of his head is not a great loss.

She is my wife and no other man's gift.

Please accept his horse to settle this rift."

AMERIGO, NOW THE GENOESE COMMANDER

"His head will stand in front of our main gate.

We all learn from his mistake and sure fate.

The right to take women will be no more.

We will live apart with an even score."

BOOK TWENTY-TWO

The Medieval Quintet: A Judge Arises from the Depths of Treachery to Restore Order and Pisan Hegemony – 1200-1260 CE

TASH

"Pisa's pulse was power proven by tact.

It sought to honor an old merchant's pact.

Its goal was to respect the people there.

It built with commerce with a laissez-faire flair."

PATTI

"Pisa guided the growth with judgement and guile.

It left alone the culture of the isle.

It found the strength new churches and roads brings.

Its role supported self-sustaining springs."

BERNADETTE

"This legacy made counts return and fight.

Ligurian lust slowly built its might.

A Tuscan hero sows peace where he could.

The Commune met its duty as it should."

MARY

"An unlikely hero would soon arise.

Cinarca's heir brought good to all's surprise.

He became judge both vigilant and fair.

He brought peace and the vendetta to bear."

CHARLOTTE

"He drew upon the future and the past.

He did well so the Pisan peace could last.

He overcame a hectic high rising tide.

But, fought often his own hubris and pride."

Cassandra Teaches Arrigo della Rocca and Ranieri Della Rocca, the Teenage Sons of Count Guido (Cinarca) della Rocca, in the Castle of Guido (Cinarca) della Rocca Near Olmeto – 1219 CE

CASSANDRA

"Your minds are like rams in the maquis' mist.

You follow some desire, not logic's twist.

Go attend to the task you want to do.

I have my own caves to find and search through."

ARRIGO DELLA ROCCA

"We Cinarchesi live life on the brink.

We take what we want with no time to think.

We must take the bride for our kin tonight.

We need more than your words for this fake fight."

CASSANDRA

"You portray a ritual many years old.

The coy bride may want to stay in the fold.

But, she parades to her own springs to drink.

They pass bond fires lighting the new link."

RANIERI DELLA ROCCA

"We want to do what Genoa has done.

In the wild Cape and down south they have won.

They reign with more ships, gold and pikes each day.

Pisa's neglect will allow them to stay."

CASSANDRA

"They live in cities behind sky high walls.

Power builds as quickly as honor falls.

They often fight if they leave their safe place.

They are islands within an island's space."

ARRIGO DELLA ROCCA

"Galleys of wood, not paper, seize the day.

We must act quickly to join the new fray.

Our power will cover all land we see.

Our safety is better than being free."

CASSANDRA

"Logic's power transcends for all ages.

Counts and mortar rise and fall in stages.

You two must soon leave to master your role.

Your duty is hollow without your soul."

RANIERI DELLA ROCCA

"Many will recall what we do this night.

As they forget Byzantium's cruel plight.

We will make good on the Pope's own order.

Genoa will rise from the southern border."

COUNT GUIDO (CINARCA) DELLA ROCCA

"My young sons have heard too many old tales.

How we lost to luck and to magic spells.

That Genoa raised us to take our land.

That the Commune must fall by our own hand."

COUNT OPIZZU DI CINARCA

"The Commune guides just one-fifth of this isle.

It is our foe which rules with tact and guile.

It joins Pisa keeping counts in their place.

My brother, we fight against a vile race."

CASSANDRA

"I hope this wedding weaves the peace you need.

Leaders from both houses must take the lead.

May culture's course fire each castle's soul.

Judgement abhors the void and loves the whole."

COUNT GUIDO (CINARCA) DELLA ROCCA

"My sons require more than heroes' deeds.

They know pain that may be cut often bleeds.

Alexander was strong as he was wise.

He won as much by force as by surprise."

COUNT OPIZZU DI CINARCA

"You train them to think as young leaders should.

They know how to act well if they just could.

They are well poised to make their novel mark.

They know their task to perform in the dark."

CASSANDRA

"I leave for the springs near your brother's house.

There to find the caverns known just to a mouse.

Hubris I fear holds their hand and their hard heart.

Yet, they too must have their own chance to start."

COUNT GUIDO (CINARCA) DELLA ROCCA

"We must all play the roles that we are given.

Tho' some may be static while some driven.

Does ritual make us think or just conform?

The dusk is the stage for us to perform."

Pascal Paul Piazza

Cassandra Travels to the Village Spring at Olmeto and Unexpectedly Meets Desiree, the Bride to Be, and Sinucellu della Rocca, Cassandra's Student and Son of Count Guglielmo della Rocca, Brother of Count Guido (Cinarca) della Rocca and Count Opizzu di Cinarca – 1219 CE

CASSANDRA

"I hope for the clear refuge for my soul.

I seek some relief from the daily dole.

Have I failed those who complete the bride quest?

They have become boorish over the best."

DESIREE

"Give wisdom, but you cannot make them think.

I am soon a bride taking my last drink.

This village spring mocks me on my grand day.

It does what it does in culture's own way."

SINUCELLU DELLA ROCCA

"I am alive, as I felt death's own grasp.

Where the boar's breath crisply cuts like a rasp.

I know the safe path that no one else know.

Look for the hidden path that logic may show."

CASSANDRA

"You see the course hubris' tact only holds.

You heed my lessons to brake stagnant molds.

Your balance of peace and harm is fragile.

Ennui still taunts your young mind so agile."

DESIREE

"I still must wed a man I have not seen.

I am still a peasant and not a queen.

Two brothers come to find me this cold night.

I must pretend to resist with my might."

SINUCELLU DELLA ROCCA

"We meet by chance at this life giving well.

We fear death as life nourishes this tale.

We approach what seems like a die so cast.

How we grow overcomes the chains of the past."

CASSANDRA

"The pupil now teaches at just age nine.

But, life must age you like a vintage wine.

I must leave as the pyres start to burn.

Good luck and know that all curves will turn."

DESIREE

"These acts unfold as they are meant to do.

I have my drink and flames show my way through.

Fires rage higher than I would expect.

Does the tender err or show some respect?

SINUCELLU DELLA ROCCA

"You are a star fixed in the black night sky.

The flames wish that they were a light so high.

You are the gift that young Pandora lost.

Search for the true goal that comes with great cost."

ANSELMO DELLA ROCCA, CAPTAIN OF THE BRIDE'S GUARD

"Your cousins soon arrive for this new bride.

Their banners unfurl and exclaim their pride.

They will act as if they must now assail.

They must attack in order to prevail."

Arrigo della Rocca and Ranieri della Rocca Invade the Castle of Their Uncle
Count Guglielmo della Rocca – 1219 CE

COUNT GUGLIELMO DELLA ROCCA

"Why do my nephews approach bearing arms?

Your armed entry would not sound the alarms.

You are here to escort a bride to wed.

Yet, you threaten me like the Moors long dead."

ARRIGO DELLA ROCCA

"Genoa first came with a wedding ruse.

This ancient ritual would serve as our fuse.

Fires do not burn for a marriage rite.

The flesh of your troops and stock burn this night."

RANIERI DELLA ROCCA

"You betray your class like some Pisan mule.

You broke your ties to Ligurian rule.

We will ravish the bride for all to see.

You cannot protect your peasants so free."

COUNT GUGLIELMO DELLA ROCCA

"I alone will fight the evil you sow.

May my blade scar you so all will know.

You cannot hide from destiny's true fate.

Your deaths are now foretold from this date."

ARRIGO DELLA ROCCA

"Release your arrows without any fear.

Then butcher him as you would a prize deer.

Find his son and draw and quarter him now.

And treat his wife like she is an old sow."

Sinucellu della Rocca Escapes and Rescues Desiree – 1219 CE

DESIREE

"Who breaks the tension of this silent room.

I cannot be seen by friends of the groom.

Does someone seek to curse me on this day?

There was not supposed to be a real fray!"

SINUCELLU DELLA ROCCA

"I dishonor you now to save your life.

Death soon consumes rather than wedding strife.

Put on your peasant clothes we all must wear.

My rectitude is my oath I now swear."

DESIREE

"What can you do, as you are nine years old?

Must I accept this as true fate foretold?

Am I not poor subject to my count's whim?

Would it not be best but to bow to him?"

SINUCELLU DELLA ROCCA

"You deserve to be free, honest and fair.

My father treated all with fulsome care.

Follow me on the paths I only know.

We will escape from dishonor so low."

DESIREE

"I am ready to follow you as I must.

You have a faith that I have learned to trust.

I tonight marry the land that is free.

Let us travel east toward the Great Sea."

Arrigo della Rocca and Ranieri della Rocca Explode that Their Troops Cannot Find Sinucellu della Rocca or Desiree – 1219 CE

ARRIGO DELLA ROCCA

"What have you not found that vile rodent child?

The paths are rock channels unlike the wild.

Straight sheer stone walls keep him fixed to the ground.

He cannot move, up, down, or around!"

RANIERI DELLA ROCCA

"He runs like a rat in a maze of stone.

He moves slowly, as he is not alone!"

Black static walls contract as they narrow.

He must feel death in his very marrow."

ANSELMO DELLA ROCCA, CAPTAIN OF THE GUARD

"Why do you chase your own cousin in flight?

The horse and dogs sense that this is not right!

How can he alone escape your whole wrath?

He is indeed on a different path!"

ARRIGO DELLA ROCCA

"Malaspina drove us from our birth-place.

We were strangers in a strange land and space.

We sought full relief from the Pope in Rome.

'Til Genoa gave us a refuge home."

RANIERI DELLA ROCCA

"We made our way back to the Southwest coast.

We imposed out rule with banners to boast.

We paid our debt to aid Genoa's gain.

Yet, my uncle sponsored the Pisan pain."

SINUCELLU DELLA ROCCA

"Moisture covers the granite face so old.

It must obscure the sterile stone so cold.

But, water, time, and plants contour the slope.

Let our feet feel the ridges with such hope."

DESIREE

"I feel safe while danger lurks around me.

While I pass on a path I cannot see.

My neck feels a breath that hardens my heart.

Feral eyes pierce my lost soul like a dart."

SINUCELLU DELLA ROCCA

"Feel each sense perched along the walls.

Low mists hide the door to the path that calls.

Trees channel us where just our stomach turns.

Fear is a fire without flame that burns."

DESIREE

"We have found the top without being found.

Up here we walk without making a sound.

How far must we go so high in the sky?

Or, should I just act now and not ask why?"

SINUCELLU DELLA ROCCA

"To not ask is to succumb to a lie.

To conform paves the path for us to die.

There is a hidden pool down from this ledge.

It will salve our thirst and our broken edge."

DESIREE

"We first met by chance at my village spring.

You brought the hope only the Sun can bring.

Your mentor taught me to let loose my fear.

It would be perfect if she were now here!"

CASSANDRA

"Why are two here drinking at this well?

Your quest here must comprise a Templar's tale.

Come rest and eat by my fire's warm light.

You had to endure a test of great fright."

DESIREE

"I have seem smoke come from this rock before.

I thought magma and water were at war.

Why do you hide in these cold caves so dark?

How can you alone help us make our mark?"

SINUCELLU DELLA ROSSA

"Her clan seeks to find the boar's baton lost.

She seeks to find our essence at all cost.

Zeus tried to hide some sons beneath the ground.

Caves conceal lost great knowledge to be found."

CASSANDRA

"I see Templar escape routes served you well.

You did hear the old lessons I did tell.

Your cousins fell prey to lust's pulsing power.

We seek the East coast at dawn's first hour."

Desiree, Cassandra, and Sinucellu della Rocca are Ambushed
at the Spring of Fiumorbo on the Road to the Costellu di Covasisa – 1219 CE

LADRU

"How arrogantly your approach our spring!

You wear no count's silk robes or golden ring.

A peasant would know how to take a drink.

Do you feel the pain being on the brink?"

DESIREE

"Why do wear dense masks and robes of bright red?

Why do you hide your face if I am so dead?

I did not come from Olmeto to die.

I will shine as stars do in the night sky."

TRUFETTU

"The stars pale when compared to your bright light.

You have endured much during your long plight.

You have had to hear our brother blather.

He often works us into a lather."

LADRU

"Let us unmask so there is no surprise.

We all live because our brother is wise.

We were to serve food for the bride to be.

He sent the alarm so we are now free."

FINADURA, MOTHER OF SINUCELLU, LADRU, AND TRUFETTU

"My nephews now drive us from our own land.

We will return one day with God's own hand.

My sons are bound to learn the Pisan way.

It is not very safe for you to stay."

Cassandra and Desiree Arrive in the Niolo Valley as It Reacts to the Rise in Power by the Counts on Either Side of the Niolo Valley – 1225 CE

STOICU

"This valley is a hive of buzzing bees.

A frenetic pace shakes the trunks of trees.

Tension ripples like circles on the lake.

Pressure builds like a dam about to break."

FERMU, PODESTA OF THE NIOLO VALLEY

"We should welcome you with our open arms.

But, we must attend all acute alarms.

We have not seen you two for a long while.

Our fights delay your feast in a grand style."

CASSANDRA

"Your plight is why we came from the East coast.

Yet, we would prefer to eat your boar roast.

The wolf now claims the banner of the Welf.

He hopes you suffer to better himself."

DESIREE

"Arrigo and Ranieri rule their land.

Their father died from shame by his own hand.

Opizzu went south with some other counts.

Genoese aid comes with fresh troops and mounts."

CASSANDRA

"They place new counts in their old homestead.

But, they seed their pain while the land has bled.

They urge Nebbiu to form a tight vise.

That you could hold out would be a surprise."

STOICU

"The Southwest-West stones fell without a test.

You block the path to the Cape from the West.

Genoa raids the East just like a Moor.

This valley must fall to open the door."

DESIREE

"You must now hold as you have always done.

This is a weary war that must be won.

They staged my wedding to complete a coup.

I have a duty of revenge just like you."

FERMU, PODESTA OF THE NIOLO VALLEY

"My troops terrace crops and their chestnut trees.

They share each other's honey from common bees.

They are resolute like trunks of a tree.

They will remain always forthright and free."

FIDELIA

"I must ask if our friends have solved the quest?

Have they found relics to help us fight best?

Has Antioch's miracle been found here?

Yet, I sense the sage course that is now clear."

CASSANDRA

"We came now as an army of just three.

We will help control the events to be.

Pisa appears to have the same belief.

Banners proclaim its army of relief."

RODRIGO, PISAN GENERAL

"It seems like we have more pure pomp than fight.

Rest assured our men deploy well with might.

Counts respond more to a banner and seal.

Those are their source of the power they feel."

VERGIL, PISAN CAPTAIN

"One thousand men go west for the defense.

A thousand more go there on the offense.

The balance will hold the main counts in place.

They must leave you alone in your own space."

OVID, A PISAN CAPTAIN

"Five hundred men go north to secure peace.

The threat of incursions will thereby cease.

The Nebbiu follows, but does not lead.

It will avoid battle if it must bleed."

FORZU, PODESTA AND REPRESENTATIVE OF THE COMMUNE

"Ships land fifteen thousand more men today.

They seek to find Arrigo in his way.

They will defeat his men and drive him back.

They will occupy his path to attack."

RODRIGO, PISAN GENERAL

"We are led by Malaspina of old.

He is retired, but his heart is bold.

We name him as judge of all of the isle.

He will guide with fairness, tact, and a smile."

Peace Council at the Castle of Arrigo della Rocca in Olmeto – 1227 CE

ISNARD MALASPINA

"We have fought these wars for almost three years.

We have seen our share of death, loss and fears.

As judge, I decree the terms of our pact.

As victor, I bestow fairness and tact."

COUNT LADRU BIONCOLACCI

"My family keeps Cinarca to rule.

We will no longer serve as someone's mule.

Our troops will now leave the Commune alone.

We again trade to show how we atone."

COUNT ARRIGO DELLA ROCCA

"My brother and I withdraw home for now.

Pisa's heel on my neck secures a bow.

Others may still hold our ancestral home.

We will return as does the sea wave's foam."

FORZU, PODESTA AND REPRESENTATIVE OF THE COMMUNE

"The need for peace curtails any sharp words.

Our pikes will again stick new cheese and curds.

Our villages remain free from a count.

While the thirst for revenge may still mount."

ISNARD MALASPINA

"I chose not to eject them as before.

We will not lose track of the cause of war.

Genoa chills the warmth of Pisan peace.

Your warm homes remain the true golden fleece."

Council of War at the Castle of Arrigo della Rocca in Olmeto – 1239 CE

COUNT RANIERI DELLA ROCCA

"Malaspina died last night in his sleep.

We must honor our promises to keep.

Pisa is cautious and will not act soon.

We will ride like ghosts in a winter moon."

COUNT ARRIGO DELLA ROCCA

"We began to prepare before he died.

We will rekindle both honor and pride.

We will ride tall under our own clan crest.

We retake all that is sacred and best."

COUNT OPIZZU CINARCA

"We will once again be one combined house.

As the Commune retreats like a scared mouse.

Cinarchesi will stir the starry sky.

Our true fortune is set as Fate's cast die."

COUNT GUGLIELMO DA MARE DI LURI

"Our sorties to the East's coast failed for years.

Our footholds were lost with much pain and tears.

This assault will dwarf the efforts before.

The whole island will entertain war."

RANIERI DELLA ROCCA

"Aleria must fear more than a raid.

It has a substantial price to be paid.

We revive the Vandals' plunder and fight.

We consume the port with metal and might."

Cassandra, Stoicu, and Desiree Witness the Assault on Aleria from the Academy – 1239 CE

STOICU

"I heard tales of the Vandals first attack.

So many black sails arranged front to back.

They had come to capture and not just raid.

That pales to the power now displayed."

DESIREE

"I was an orphan that this port took in.

It nourished my redemption from my sin.

Our defense may start to help me repay.

Wisdom and guile will surely show the way."

CASSANDRA

"I am proud that tact guides us to stay in place.

The Commune needs an anchor in this space,

We can delay their march rather than hide.

We will engage them with judgement and pride."

COUNT GUGLIELMO BIANCALACCI

"The school is a spleen spewing Pisan bile.

We must exorcise these demons so vile.

These three should feel the weight of iron chains.

Sulphur burns hotter when Greek fire rains."

ADMIRAL ARTURO DORIA OF GENOA

"Enough, your vengeance is not our current plan.

We are not the vanguard of a hurt clan.

The Commune needs its links to eastern trade.

If we hold this port, its prospects will fade."

DESIRE

"You treat this island like a new trade right.

Commerce's concession to pay while we fight.

These counts you trust do not wear the red cross.

They are jackals laughing at your troops' loss."

ADMIRAL ARTURO DORIA OF GENOA

"Moor and Christian fight and we trade with each.

Profits from trade is the lesson we teach.

You know the true precedent of the past.

Our quarters help make emir and count last."

CASSANDRA

"Your perfidy is an accepted fact.

But what have you learned from each soul-less pact?

Your anchor cannot grasp our solid stone.

Our rectitude and tack stand alone."

ADMIRAL ARTURO DORIA OF GENOA

"I can provide a lost magical text.

It may ask if what you teach is pretext.

Trade aside, we come to learn how to rule.

Is that not the purpose of this old school?"

STOICU

"Do you know where a child of Zeus did kneel?

Where does the sky open to become real?

You tempt, but that is not how the mind's cog turns.

Your deceit is a flame eating what it burns."

**Cassandra, Stoicu, and Desiree Meet with Admiral Arturo Doria of Genoa
as Pisa Recaptures Aleria – 1241 CE**

ADMIRAL ARTURO DORIA OF GENOA

"The Commune is a chestnut still intact.

Secure through your spying as well as tact.

New markets open both Christian and Moor.

We shall be gone from this desolate shore."

CASSANDRA

"So, you join Thibault in a new crusade.

I hope our lessons were not a charade.

Our message was very profound and sage.

It extends beyond time and any age."

DESIREE

"You did not learn how to mix with peasants.

High walls hid a flock of Persian pheasants.

For commerce, you have no known rival.

Deceit is not the soul of survival."

STOICU

"I still wait for the ancient book I lack.

A milestone for such stars to change our tack.

The Templars found treasure in old caves.

You leave us empty on the wind and waves."

ADMIRAL ARTURO DORIA OF GENOA

"Pisa's banners unfurl in the bright sky.

I hold my own gift to know to ask why.

I leave no manuscript for you to leer.

That I know more about that text is clear."

Meria
Brandu
Munticellu
Bastia
Nebbiu
Biguglia
Balange
Loretu
Mariana
Calvi
Filiceto
Niolo Valley
Aleria
Aitone Forest
Cinarca
Bocca di San Ghjoghju
Aiacciu
Filitosa
Olmeto
Propriano
Bonifaziu

The Cycle of Cyrnos
Sinucellu della Rocca, Unknown to Desiree and Dressed as a Pisan Captain,
Approaches Desiree Who Does Not Recognize Him, Cassandra, Who Does Recognize Him,
and Stoicu at the Village Spring in Merusaglia – 1245 CE

SINUCELLU DELLA ROCCA

"Does this spring mock you as other have done?

Or, does your thirst quench with such battles won?

Do you so mirror the pulseless cold stone?

Must I leave such a strong woman alone?"

DESIREE

"A true Pisan captain knows how to act!

He would be guided by honor and tact.

Your questions are those that a friend would ask.

But, I still do not know your present task."

CASSANDRA

"Your wry wit returns to when we first met.

You did not truly know everything yet.

We curse caprice's whim when your father died.

Hope lives inside if not truly outside."

STOICU

"Villages lament their recent freedoms lost.

The Genoese gambit came with such cost.

We were a ship listing without an oar.

Yet, we were like strong birds ready to soar."

FORZU, PODESTA AND REPRESENTATIVE OF THE COMMUNE

"Pisa has restored the strength and order.

Its troops now protect the Commune's border.

They will be led by a new judge to be.

We will again be honest, fervent, and free."

GENERAL RODRIGO OF PISA

"We campaign by war or peace as we must.

We draw upon the island's faith and trust.

Our new judge hales from the Corsican land.

He will guide us with a fair, firm and free hand."

SINUCELLU DELLA ROCCA NOW GHJUDICE DELLA ROCCA

"I accept the duty of judge for all.

I was taught well when I was very small.

I serve from the terraces to the Sea.

The maquis wants us to be honest and free."

CASSANDRA

"I now know what Aristotle did fear.

Did I make a monster or a great peer.

I am too old to see this story end.

I know you have a faith that will not bend."

DESIREE

"You just saved me when no one else did so.

I was like wheat chaff left never to sow.

Yet, for you, I have grown to reach my best.

Now, your friends and you face the toughest test."

GHJUDICE DELLA ROCCA

"I was a captain just in the right place.

I did not let the French take Pisan space.

I am no Caesar in Britain or Gaul.

I am a native judge working for all."

The Cycle of Cyrnos

Count Arrigo della Rocca, Count Ranieri della Rocca, and Count Opizzu di Cinarca
Meet at the Castle of Count Arrigo della Rocca to Plot the War Against Their Cousin Ghjudice della
Rocca, Pisa, and the Commune in Olmeto – 1245 CE

COUNT OPIZZU DI CINARCA

"Bonifaziu's cliffs keep us secure.

Our clan there will resist and not abjure.

You each have a castle that stands alone.

There will be such a bold blood killing zone."

COUNT ARRIGO DELLA ROCCA

"He will invest us first to start the war.

He will plunge headlong like a rabid boar.

He will want to kill me with his own hand.

We know how to hunt the boar on our land."

COUNT RANIERI DELLA ROCCA

"The Gorges open him up to defeat.

The northern counts will feign a full retreat.

They will not defend the passes of stone.

He then moves South to attack us alone."

COUNT ARRIGO DELLA ROCCA

"Once through the rocks we will pick where to fight.

There his two cousins appear in his sight.

Embers of anger fuel his fulsome hate.

His men will then move fast, sure, and straight."

COUNT RANIERI DELLA ROCCA

"Our Genoese pike will be hard to break.

He is like a hurt boar tied to a stake.

Then the northern troops attack en masse.

And a strong, complete win will come to pass."

171

Ghjudice della Rocca and His Brothers, Ladru and Trufettu, Marshal Their Troops and the Pisan Army as the Bocca di San Ghjoghju Which Separate the Northern Counts from the Southern Counts and is The Main Pass Between North and South and Where Ghjudice della Rocca Must Pass – 1245 CE

LADRU

"The Biancalacci hide in their halls.

They fear the Cinarchesi clan soon falls.

The open passes are a die now cast.

We must do as Caesar did in the past."

TRUFETTU

"Each pass is where sheer rocks and earth did rift.

A defenseless pass is a martial gift.

We know three-hundred could defend this way.

We could make it secure this very day."

GHJUDICE DELLA ROCCA

"Spineless men may hide, but they still have arms.

They are not peasants restored to their farms.

We will deploy where we know that we can.

We must continue to follow our plan."

LADRU

"I will signal the shadow Pisan fleet.

They provide men, supplies, and food to eat.

The reserve's strong song is music so sweet.

Let the counts in the north feign a retreat."

TRUFETTU

"We will proceed as designed at all cost.

Ours is a pure cause that is not soon lost.

We do not need banners, legends, or lore.

We are a true band of brothers at war."

Count Guglielmo Biancalacci, Count Ladru Biancalacci, and Count Ghjudecellu Biancalacci Rebuke the Entreaties of Trufettu on Behalf of Ghjudice della Rocca and Begin the War – 1245 CE

COUNT GUGLIELMO BIANCALACCI

"My family has raised one-thousand men.

You are a few old goats caught in a pen.

You cannot stop us from striking the host.

An impaling the judge's head on a post."

TRUFETTU

"Why do you think your maneuvers confuse?

We know your retreat is simply a ruse.

We will not let you hereafter attack.

It is your homes that we soon seek to sack."

COUNT LADRU BIANCALACCI

"You speak bravely for a man quick to die.

Do you think that we would believe your lie?

Return to your men and make peace with God.

We will wade waist deep in blood on the sod."

COUNT GHJUDECELLU BIANCALACCI

"It is just and right we beat this defense.

God wills that we move south for offense.

Sound the horn and waive the banner to start.

We move en masse to watch you now depart."

COUNT GUGLIELMO BIANCALACCI

"Why are our troops static and stuck in place.

Why do our ranks start to collapse in space?

Order fails as bodies start to pile high.

But, for God's mercy we will all soon die."

COUNT LADRU BIANCALACCI

"God will send no legion to save our soul.

The judge did not head south with the main whole.

His ranks swell with four times as many men.

We are the ones caught dead in our own pen."

COUNT GHJUDECELLU BIANCALACCI

"Sound the horn and strike the banners today.

No more should die for our hubris at play.

We are still Corsicans and not vile Moors.

We seek a fair and just judgment of wars."

GHJUDICE DELLA ROCCA

"I will accept a soldier's terms this night.

Let us end quickly now this needless fight.

Find your own wives and children asleep.

They need not to have a reason to weep."

LADRU

"Your castles rooks will be secure once more.

But, no village must supply men for war.

Each person shall be free to work the land.

Contracts to till will rule not power's hand."

TRUFETTU

"A count's innate rights died in this blood field.

Peasants may support, but need not yield.

Genoese ships also met with defeat.

They now return home with the Pisan fleet."

Count Arrigo della Rocca, Count Ranieri della Rocca, and Madonna Sibila React to the Defeat of the Northern Counts and Their Plan to Defeat the Ghjudice della Rocca in Olmeto – 1245 CE

MADONNA SIBILA

"You were too causal to wage war this day.

You thought my bed prepared you for the fray.

You are fearless with your men around.

Your hubris was blind to facts on the ground."

COUNT ARRIGO DELLA ROCCA

"He came to the great gorge just like he should.

He sent the first three-hundred through as he could.

His flags ignored the northern counts that fled.

It was the judge in front who bravely led."

COUNT RANIERI DELLA ROCCA

"He should soon be through with his complete host.

His flanks and rear guard should be exposed most.

But, the vanguard was there to hold the gate.

His full strength went north to decide its fate."

MADONNA SIBILA

"The judge plotted a sage and solid course.

He did not rashly move his pike and horse.

He did not see the gorge as his sole path.

Rather, a split foe would feel his whole wrath."

COUNT RANIERI DELLA ROCCA

"We held our ground with a fervor so bold.

We could only watch the events unfold.

We were deployed to contract the steel vise.

Which the judge did to the lost counts' surprise."

COUNT ARRIGO DELLA ROCCA

"His passion for revenge remains still strong.

But, forgetting his clever mind was wrong.

His wit saved him when he was a young child.

Just as his hot temper could make him wild."

COUNT RANIERI DELLA ROCCA

"He has thought beyond the lessons of old.

He can tell the peasants that iron is gold.

The northern counts abjure to Pisa's soul.

Their supine succor supplants their own soul."

COUNT ARRIGO DELLA ROCCA

"We will not suffer these lost northern fools.

Our cause is lost as long as Pisa rules.

We can scheme now to tempt his love or lore.

His weakness is a woman and not war."

COUNT RANIERI DELLA ROCCA

"He has dark skin and peasant chestnut hair.

He is short with random features just fair.

His profile tempts so few women to grasp.

What woman seeks someone so rough and rasp?"

MADONNA SIBILA

"Your brother finally has a true insight.

We now have a plan bold, brilliant and bright.

The judge's fall is a spectacle to see.

Leave the woman's wiles and cunning to me!"

**Ghjudice della Rocca Accepts an Invitation to Dine with Madonna Sibila
Who Extends an Offer of Marriage – 1245 CE**

MADONNA SIBILA

"I did not think I would be well received.

You must have thought that you would be deceived.

But, let us eat a meal of wine and bread.

I must know if you are alive or dead."

GHJUDICE DELLA ROCCA

"I had to hear what a sybil might say.

Your words may foretell my purpose this day.

Will you guide me past my father's own grave?

Or disclose whose soul I may or may not save?"

MADONNA SIBILA

"My soul is the Genoese clever class.

I find joy in a bed or at a Mass.

My late spouse came here to aid the counts' rise.

Yet, now I can give you a greater surprise."

GHJUDICE DELLA ROCCA

"You balance among foes in the middle.

You weave your own path with a rogue riddle.

You reach out to start a new raucous race.

What plots concoct behind that luring face?"

MADONNA SIBILA

"Marry me to stop the carnage and lust.

Our union is one that all can trust.

Except for now where tears fall like rains.

Guards, honor Circe, and put him in chains."

GHJUDICE DELLA ROCCA

"Did Circe reveal that she fully lost?

Did she disclose the acute pain it cost?

I have been captive in a colder cell.

Your ruse fails, as I can survive in Hell."

MADONNA SIBILA

"Each hour parades what you cannot touch.

Napes, breast and thighs that tempt you so much.

Birds will peck your flesh to find your liver.

This is pure pain revenge will deliver."

GHJUDICE DELLA ROCCA

"What, no rock to roll up a hill this day?

No fruit beyond grasp to cause dismay?

The eagle stays to talk and not to eat!

The hourly display is a lustful treat!"

MADONNA SIBILA

"You will pay as Aeneas did not do.

You will not found a new brazen race too.

You will feel pain's pangs worse than Dido felt.

Your cousins apply each bruise, gash, and welt."

GHJUDICE

"My cousins could not catch me at age nine.

Why should I fear the timbre of their whine?

I can leave at my whim and when I care.

Please leave me to meditate if you dare."

DESIREE

"I hear you killed ten men with just one blade.

Yet, you cannot overcome the trap you made!

Would you like me to show you the way out?

Just follow the thread to where the plants sprout."

GHJUDICE

"The tables fast turn in more than one way.

The beast in the maze should not leave but stay.

You rescue me, as I once did for you.

You found paths when others were not true."

DESIREE

"As a maid's daughter, I knew the whole house.

My real teacher was a clever white mouse.

I soon found all of the secrets inside.

Including, all the good paths to hide."

GHJUDICE DELLA ROCCA

"I was as blind as hubris could forsake.

I must learn from this woeful itch's mistake.

You were taken to serve a heavy hand.

I must return all peasants to the land."

DESIREE

"You freed me when no one else would or could.

You have no debt to pay in wax or wood.

Just be the just judge we know you can be.

Counts can be counts; peasants can be free."

Madonna Sibila Excoriates Ladru and Trufettu About Their Absent Brother Not Knowing that Desiree Had Rescued Ghjudice della Rocca

MADONNA SIBILA

"Where is your brother when we need him most?

Your cousins march closer to match their boast.

What good is a judge's win that is lost in bile?

Call Hector and not a dog with a smile."

TRUFETTU

"You seem to know when our cousins arrive.

That their vast army will help you survive.

You should know where our lost brother may be.

He left for your villa joking carefree."

GHJUDICE

"You look like you have seen a ghost at night.

My cousins' headless vanguard knows your fright.

Hubris' servile chains no longer bind me.

I start my campaign for us to be free."

LADRU

"Impaled heads on pikes make a gruesome sight.

The gauntlet path showed our fulsome might.

Our cousins' main host did not laugh or boast.

They withdrew quickly to the Southwest coast."

GHJUDICE

"Your deceit deserves its own special prize.

You can dance naked without a surprise.

Your new house will allow you to be free.

While your madame will reap a higher fee."

Illustration: Mouflon of Corsica — The Litz Collection

BOOK TWENTY-THREE

The Medieval Quintet: The Corsican Interlude Comes to an End Along with the Pisan Peace and the Official Crusading Movement – 1245-1307 CE

TASH

"Pisa was steward for two-hundred years.

It stood out for fairness submerging fears.

The Pisan Peace arc came to its own end.

Genoese force caused its downward bend."

PATTI

"The Crusades commenced with Claremont's cold call.

After two-centuries Outremer would fall.

This isle's traits tested the movement's true soul.

From skeptic to Templar, it served the whole."

BERNADETTE

"The judge was advocate for sixty years.

He set the standard for the isle's peers.

The Commune and people were one strong block.

The counts faked a feud to build their own stock."

MARY

"Genoa used the feud to take more land.

Its troops though fell to the judge's skillful hand.

The judge would fall to mixed deceit and pride.

While the baton's search saw a intrigued ride."

CHARLOTTE

"This interlude built on the bedrock past.

It was the die that character did cast.

Rectitude would soon face Genoese pain.

Looking to patriots to break the chain."

The Niolo Valley Prepares for the Assembly in Merusaglia – 1249 CE

AUDACE

"The judge asks for the whole Commune to meet.

Are we to honor him over the counts' defeat?

Will he use this chance to become a king?

Are we Brutus fated to stop this thing?"

URSA

"Why do you bother me with such nonsense?

He puts on no air and makes no pretense!

Rather, ask where does the baton now rest?

I have no answer to that riddle's test!"

AUDACE

"You ignore a new coup for some token.

I care that the counts' old chains are broken.

I oppose any tack to make us less free.

We must be ready to sting like a bee."

URSA

"The answer came from a lost Greek now found.

Hercules forms each night and bends unbound.

He kneels above Genoa on one knee.

He provides the home star over the Sea."

AUDACE

"Genoese perfidy knows no known bound.

Their ships come from the East making no sound.

They dress like Moors to open the trade doors.

Their goal was profit from the lasting wars."

Ghjudice della Rocca, Fieru, Podesta from the Niolo Valley, Audace, and Ursa Travel to Merusaglia – 1249 CE

GHJUDICE DELLA ROCCA (DRESSED AS A MONK)

"May a barefoot monk join your path this day?

I promise that I will have little to say.

Your podesta and you seem resolute.

What quest lures you on this bare rocky route?"

FIERU, PODESTA OF THE NIOLO VALLEY

"The Commune convenes to set our new path.

Many peasants have been saved from an old wrath.

I come to aid our new judge in that role.

He must learn to draw from the complete whole."

AUDACE

"He may think that he alone is the best.

But, he cannot be better than the rest.

His power will never make us less free.

He must now balance like waves of the sea."

URSA

"The search for the baton must change its tack.

That is the key and not some counts' attack.

He was taught by a great teacher of old.

He will know the events that must unfold."

GHJUDICE DELLA ROCCA (DRESSED AS A MONK)

"He was taught by such a sage steady hand.

Who, in turn, sought the baton in this land.

He is not blind to both key pursuits.

Or the need to follow diverging routes."

URSA

"The road is silent that the judge arrives.

None of Rome's grand pomp or glory survives.

There are no flags, music or cheering crowd.

The donkey's brash bray is the sound most loud."

FIERU, PODESTA OF THE NIOLO VALLEY

"Each podesta is here set to convene.

But, the judge is absent yet to be seen.

We will still debate his role and our needs.

We will cultivate freedom's fulsome seeds."

AUDACE

"We, like the stones and maquis, play our role.

The terrace rows satisfy our free soul.

How do you know what motivates this man?

He commands for praise and a sense of elan."

URSA

"Recall the path that the great Godfrey took.

He came to the City as sinners look.

Prostrate and barefoot he wore no gold ring.

He would rule by tact and not as a king."

GHJUDICE DELLA ROCCA (DRESSED A MONK)

"Let this poor monk humbly kneel at your feet.

I am the vanguard of the counts' defeat.

As advocate, and not king, I will rule.

I will be the judge I was taught in school."

FIERU, PODESTA OF THE NIOLO VALLEY

"Fairness and justice is what we will need.

Only that skill will counter the counts' greed.

We will combine all our freeholding land.

Which we shape with our judgement and our hand."

URSA

"We need to find the baton that is lost.

We must not be afraid to bear such cost.

Genoa remains a thorn in our side.

Its theft of the baton punctures our pride."

AUDACE

"Quiet, he has real bold burdens to bear.

He is forgiven if he does not care.

He must pursue the tasks that he deems best.

And which is not your esoteric quest."

FIERU, PODESTA OF THE NIOLO VALLEY

"We welcome your guard, but please let her speak.

Our brother hears what each of you may seek.

He is judge for all your ideas you may think.

The chain breaks, but do not form a new link."

GHJUDICE DELLA ROCCA (DRESSED AS A MONK)

"I can speak well by myself when I must.

We will build bridges and churches to build trust.

We seek to expunge Cinarchesi lust.

And, we aid her search before the stars burst."

URSA

"Pisa was grateful for his martial deeds.

They made him judge to meet our current needs.

His arrogance and hubris do resound.

Still, there is tact and fairness to be found."

AUDACE

"Do we know who challenged him to ask?

Yet, he must provide answers for our task.

Can we trust he knows what we are about?

A victor from the counts line gives me doubt."

URSA

"Cassandra set the compass of his mind.

The standing stones gave him a soul to find.

He knew there was more than the stones to see.

That they remind us that we must be free."

AUDACE

"Can megaliths fill up an empty heart?

When will his martial greed for power start?

I hear he is weak for a woman's touch.

That does not placate my full fears too much."

URSA

"Ulisse had no peer for his keen wit

Yet, he could succumb to combat's deep pit.

Women were his bane and gave him great gifts.

He, like the judge, can heal the moral rifts."

Meeting of Counts in the Cap Corse at the Costellu de Mare – 1250 CE

COUNT ALDO BIANDI DU CAPI DI LURI

"The Cap Corse is such a precocious child.

Untold potential while remaining wild.

We two counts divide the spoils in like kind.

The judge and the Commune pay us no mind."

COUNT GUGLIELMO DI MARE

"Defeat made some counts pledge to Pisan lords.

Fear compels them to sheath their hidden swords.

We mark our own course under our tower.

We build in stealth Liguria's power."

COUNT ALDO BIANDI DU CAPI DI LURI

"You still speak plainly of the truest course.

We await to unleash such a fierce force.

I cede all my land and rights just to you.

You are free to rule strongly as you do."

COUNT GUGLIELMO DI MARE

"Your gift of Brandu's caves starts my campaign.

I can find Deb's books and rule with disdain.

We have the baton, but no books in hand.

But, just Ursa knows where to search this land."

LUCCA, DESCENDENT CORSICAN TEMPLAR

"My brother and I have devised a ruse.

I have an offer she cannot refuse.

She must trust a native Templar's vow.

She will reveal the books and humbly bow."

**Mateu and Lucca, Descendent Corsican Templars Approach Ursa at Her Academy
in Aleria Being Managed by Master Alibi – 1250 CE**

MATEU, DESCENDENT CORSICAN TEMPLAR

"We search for a teacher, Ursa, by name.

We come to honor her judgement and fame.

We need a mentor for our master's son.

Folly ensnares him and must be undone."

MASTER ALIBI

"Usually, you would not find her here.

But, she arrived this morning with great cheer.

She lacks interest in any offer.

Plus, there is no known gift you can proffer."

LUCCA, DESCENDENT CORSICAN TEMPLAR

"We know she solved the baton's riddle best.

Templar intrigue started her on her quest.

She cannot ignore the red cross's allure.

Her insightful mind must follow the lure."

URSA

"Am I smart if I accept lead for gold?

Am I keen if I fall for each tale told?

Am I a moth caught by the light's low glow?

I do not know what you think I may know."

MATEU, DESCENDENT CORSICAN TEMPLAR

"Your mental Gordian know will not hold.

You win when you wield a sharp mind so bold.

Like Alexander, the sword cuts all knots.

Bind and gag her next to the ship's clay pots."

Erbulunga

Brandu – (Costellu)

Mateu and Lucca, the Descendent Corsican Templars, Deliver Ursa and Audace to Guglielmo du Mare in Brandu at the Village of Erbulunga – 1250 CE

GUGLIELMO DI MARE

"This is the mystic whose knowledge is key?

She taps the force of an eagle and bee?

You quelch her power by keeping her bound.

You have subdued her to the stony ground."

MATEU, DESCENDENT CORSICAN TEMPLAR

"She is not worse for wear withs rasps and scrapes.

She had to be bound to prevent her escapes.

She did not take your offer to be here..

She just needs some sleep to find her lost cheer."

LUCCA, DESCENDENT CORSICAN TEMPLAR

"We will take her to Costellu this night.

At sunrise, she leads our team without fright.

She will not be bound within the cave walls.

She must be alert as a cave façade falls."

URSA

"You two bravely caught a maid at no cost.

I now can see how Outremer was lost.

Even when bound, I am still fully free.

You will never get any help from me."

GUGLIELMO DI MARE

"I will miss the glow of her temper's sparks.

She so engages with both bile and bark.

I may be gone, but I leave you a gift.

I stole her friend so there would be no rift."

Mateu and Lucca, the Descendent Corsican Templars, and Ursa Enter the Caves Located Outside the Mountain Village of Costellu in Brandu – 1250 CE

URSA

"Quiet, they still sleep in stupor and sloth.

We can fake our profile under this cloth.

We will hide in the caves beyond their view.

We will leave when their search for us is through."

AUDACE

"I do not know why you like caves so dark.

We should run to and not from the fire's spark.

But, your plan makes sense in a clever way.

Yet, I hope they stop in less than a day."

URSU

"This looks like an oviu of the South.

But, it is an unlikely cave's mouth.

Thirty feet back looks like a strong stone wall.

A narrow gap though runs both firm and tall."

AUDACE

"Yet, it does not seem we could pass through here.

All the rock wall faces are cold and shear.

A slender way forces our backs to stone.

The air is viscous while we are alone."

URSA

"We move sideways on the walls so damp.

We cannot turn, but I see a faint lamp.

Keep your hand on my hip as we step slow.

Be ready to maneuver and duck low."

AUDACE

"You are the badger re-tracing its path.

You feel hope when I just touch woe and wrath.

You project that the wall will have a door.

When cut stone shows claws but no door before."

URSA

"I know this geometry in my mind.

The elusive route is so hard to find.

The trompe l'oeil contours a path to deceive.

What is real is what we cannot perceive!"

AUDACE

"You are calm while we receive this harm's way.

But, what now cracks and invokes fear today?

My neck hair bristle from a surly growl.

The pungent breath belies a wise old owl."

URSA

"Two coal eyes await our way on this wall.

The ceiling lowers as the head seems tall.

Cerberus must guard the entrance himself.

Time to put your doubt and fear on the shelf."

AUDACE

"I shake as if the dream walkers arrive.

Logic and faith meet to try to survive.

It is not that I am frozen in place.

A sharp tooth forces me forward in space."

LUCCA, DESCENDENT CORSICAN TEMPLAR

"Our pikes pierce, point and push you still unbound.

You may not crawl back from the growling sound.

You cast the die when you withdrew alone.

You must act fast if you are to atone."

A TALKING CERBERUS WITH SNAKE HAIR

"I am the labor Hercules refused.

I left Daedalus lost and confused.

I share the Gorgons' power to scare.

What vile creatures dare enter my lair?"

URSA

"Yet, I see Athena's judgment so wise.

And Artemis's skill with stags I surmise!

You can change shape when you figure you must.

You just require us to show our trust."

AUDACE

"Let me face this beast as best that I can.

I see one who hates both woman and man.

We can receive a sharp stab in the back,

Or, withstand now this ugly beast's attack."

LUCCA, DESCENDENT CORSICAN TEMPLAR

"What role we play still remains your own choice.

Outside the cave, the troops soon will rejoice.

They know the terror of the beast inside.

The horror consumes both hubris and pride."

A TALKING CERBERUS WITH SNAKE HAIR

"Come feel my cloak made from others like you.

My canines lust for your jugular too.

Your sweat reveals the fear that you now hide.

Watch me pounce on your frail hope that has died."

AUDACE

"How can you jump so agile, strong and fast?

I know of no such vile beast from the past.

Help me as a Templar swears he would do.

Is the oath a lie or is it still true?"

MATEU, DESCENDENT CORSICAN TEMPLAR

"Now you seek our assistance and our help.

Your discourse replaces logic with a yelp.

I stand on my oath before God and man.

I will save the beast as best that I can."

A TALKING CERBERUS WITH SNAKE HAIR

"Your flesh is my meal I savor this night.

My claws slowly pursue your pulsing fright.

Wait, why does not your old friend try to fight?

Will she just let me ravage you tonight?"

URSA

"You have Gorgon hair, yet are we not stone?

A jackal dog will not act alone.

My friend is safe and remains ever so free.

I still wait to see what I cannot see!"

DEB (REVEALING HERSELF AS THE TALKING CERBERUS WITH SNAKE HAIR)

"It is now time for this charade to end.

We had to see if you would break or bend.

You are truly the ones to make this quest.

And see through the facade we made best."

Lucca, an Descendent Corsican Templar

"We must pretend you were captives at bay.

Where just Templars can guide the enclosed way.

The count's men all fear to enter this cave.

So, you enter the beast's lair and your grave."

MATEU, DESCENDENT CORSICAN TEMPLAR

"We guard Deb's books so they will not be found.

They are safe under the count's nose and ground.

The baton lies dormant across the sea.

Its power fades without the books' old key."

URSA

"So, for years we could not pass this old test.

We were in a sure trap with all the rest.

Now, we join to protect Deb's own gift.

And help pretend the schist strata can shift."

AUDACE

"While you all may laugh, my heart felt acute pain.

I do not know which one of you is sane.

Fear made my bones feel like fractured egg shells.

Why does hurt result in these Templar tales?"

MATEU, DESCENDENT CORSICAN TEMPLAR

"We and you descend from a unique line.

Our trails go back to that Cypriot mine.

Lucca taught Anna always to persist.

Daedalus proved to her Deb's books do exist."

LUCCA, DESCENDENT CORSICAN TEMPLAR

"From then, our fates have been integrally bound.

We were the paradox of paths unwound.

You sought a known staff that could not be found.

Just to find lost books that I kept underground."

DEB

"These three metal tablets hold books so bold.

They are a guide for power to unfold.

But, just the baton can direct their force.

And keep the rule of our culture on course."

URSA

"I can read the inlaid symbols still new.

They describe the Corsican traits so true.

Rectitude, fairness and honor unbound.

They are the full tone to freedom's true sound."

DEB

"Liguria's lust must be kept at bay.

What is at stake is the Corsican way.

The baton and books must be kept apart.

Or, my dear that is when real pain will start."

Jacapo Doria, a Genoese Diplomat, and Massimo Doria, a Genoese General, Plead with Ranieri della Rocca to Leave for Genoa Since the Judge has Had His Brother, Arrigo della Rocca, Poisoned and Has Been Sieging Ranieri della Rocca During a Visit to the Costellu della Rocca in Olmeto – 1257 CE

JACAPO DORIA, GENOAN DIPLOMAT

"Your brother had a woman in his bed.

That was normal, except now he is dead.

She died from the same poison I dread.

The judge's reach can kill anyone it is said."

MASSIMO DORIA, GENOAN GENERAL

"For five years you sit captive under siege.

Your subjects join the judge calling him liege.

Escape to Genoa while you still can.

I will make peace as part of our plan."

RANIERI DELLA ROCCA

"I will not leave like a thief in the night.

I am not an old bear failing to fight.

My banner remains high for forty years.

I will not replace hubris with my tears."

JACAPO DORIA, GENOAN DIPLOMAT

"We will escort you under your high flag.

Your profile juts strong like a shear rock crag.

Your clan once found refuge in my homeland.

Return to Genoa for days so grand."

MASSIMO DORIA, GENOESE GENERAL

"Your brother heads south to his own refuge.

Our colony there withstand the deluge.

Lesser counts call Cinarchesi land home.

Their stay is short while their dead spirits roam."

Ghjudice della Rocca, Trufettu della Rocca and Ladru della Rocca Watch as Ranieri della Rocca and the Genoese Party Withdraw from Olmeto for Genoa – 1257 CE

TRUFETTU DELLA ROCCA

"Why do we watch as Ranieri escapes?

He celebrates on wine from our grapes.

Our father cringes at this eerie sight.

Let us unleash our overwhelming might."

GHJUDICE DELLA ROCCA

"For ten years we have only known these wars.

Our goal now is not to even the scores.

Each village now can achieve its own best.

We have met our vow on this robust quest."

LADRU DELLA ROCCA

"Our old long lost home is ready once more.

Our father's honor returns to its past lore.

We are the tortoise winning the long race.

The hare retires from this sacred place."

GHJUDICE DELLA ROCCA

"This day is the goal of related acts.

Brought about by a series of sure pacts.

He will feel the vendetta's purest sting.

Just as father now returns to his spring."

LADRU DELLA ROCCA

"Plans unfurl easy in logic's tower.

Practice finds pain in the use of power.

No attack can be a powerful tool.

From that void comes a righteous and fair rule."

After Poisoning Arrigo della Rocca Rather than Attacking Him, After Allowing Ranieri della Rocca to Withdraw to Genoa, and Placating the Remaining Lesser Counts, Ghjudice della Rocca Defends His Actions and Inactions to Desiree, Hanna, Ursa, Raymond of Albi (Whose Group of Albigensians Relocated to Southwest Corsia After the Albigensian Crusade) at the Restored Castle in Olmeto – 1257 CE

HANNA

"Does the shepherd stall neglecting his flock?

Tensions churn like magma under the rock.

Northern counts chafe ready for battle.

Genoa's disdain treats us like chattel."

GHJUDICE DELLA ROCCA

"I was taught that tact served leaders much more.

His City just fell by pact and not war!

I deal with counts as Outremer did too.

The results are so time tested and true."

HANNA

"Blind tactics are not a true tiller's tack.

It projects peace when troops wait to attack.

A surprise attack will make masses move.

Random pieces need a proper steady grove."

GHJUDICE DELLA ROCCA

"People need not deal with the counts' hand.

They are left alone to do with their land.

Too much blood and death had to be spent.

There must be a new message that is sent."

HANNA

"Our character is the maquis and stone.

Fairness and tact keep us strong alone.

Mystery also helps compose the way.

A judge's deeds speak louder than words can say."

URSA

"Many foes now ally to dilute our traits.

Genoa lurks in ports, valleys and straights.

Kings make plans not to build, but to subvert.

The Pope just cares about power to exert."

HANNA

"Our links span from the Ebro to Marseilles.

Standing stones, pots and trade set the way.

But, Lange d'oc ceases to be anymore.

Freedom has been crushed to even a score."

DESIREE

"The last three Crusades bypassed both our shores.

Southwest France was besieged by the Pope's wars.

Free Toulouse fell now lost in Louis' ring.

Aragon withdraws under its young king."

RAYMOND OF ALBI

"We left Albi once again to be free.

But, the counts' firm yoke choked our hopes to be.

The judge has made the counts yield to our goal.

But, we need much more that just our own soul."

GHJUDICE DELLA ROCCA

"The counts withdraw so our culture rises.

I have done my part with no surprises.

Why can't I produce my own proper heir?

And honor our father with sons who care?"

Pascal Paul Piazza

Ghjudice della Rocca Entertains Ibn Waisel, Envoy of Baibars (the Mameluke Ruler who Retook Jerusalem) and Jacapo Doria, Genoese Diplomat, After They Were Received by the Holy Roman Emperor Conrad and Were Returning to the Holy Land – 1258 CE

IBN WAISEL, ENVOY OF BAIBARS

"You Franks are not what you image conveys.

Short and dark are not what a judge portrays.

Yet, we all comprise Avicenna's tree.

Wisdom and reason keep all of us free."

GHJUDICE DELLA ROCCA

"So, do I have some worth if put to a bid?

Why do you claim that my talents are hid?

You are an envoy fresh from Manfred's court.

Your master Baibars sends words that contort."

IBN WAISEL, ENVOY OF BAIBARS

"You do not embrace the gifts God bestows.

You are static like your standing stone rows.

Preston John will not deploy in your ranks.

There is no one else but God to give thanks."

GHJUDICE DELLA ROCCA

"Your master rose from just a slave at birth.

His martial skill elevated his true worth.

He outsmarts all counts and emirs alike.

He knows when to confer and when to strike."

IBN WAISEL, ENVOY OF BAIBARS

"Yes, you took the City by a pact's grace.

Which, in turn enraged the whole Muslim race.

Peace with counts helped neither crescent nor cross.

Baibars holds the City to your great loss."

JACAPO DORIA, GENOESE DIPLOMAT

"Genoa seeks your homage at no cost.

Just think of the fresh troops soon to be lost.

We will not give up 'til we win the war.

And, there will be more bloody fights in store."

GHJUDICE DELLA ROCCA

"One more envoy with words that I must hear.

Golden promises of peace so near.

I may be weary, but my eyes still see.

Your pact does not promise we will be free."

JACAPO DORIA, GENOESE DIPLOMAT

"I attend at your brother's own request.

To sow the seeds of success of your quest.

We came to hear what you may now suggest.

We can guide with a plan that we know best."

GHJUDICE DELLA ROCCA

"My brother acts as I ask him to do.

He flushes out the quail when we are through.

The rocks form layers laid out in the past.

Genoa can be in the strata cast."

IBN WAISEL, ENVOY OF BAIBARS

"Delphi would long envy the words you said.

Is the Pisan peace still alive or dead?

Each ear will hear just what it wants to hear.

My master sends his praise, wishes and cheer."

Ghjudice della Rossa and Trufettu della Rossa Discuss the Meeting with Ibn Waisel, Envoy of Baibars, and Jacapo Doria, Genoese Diplomat, in the Family Home in Olmeto – 1258 CE

GHJUDICE DELLA ROSSA

"You were right to ask the Genoese here.

We will have more control if they stay near.

Ladru remains to engage them each day.

He may renew my pledge in our own way."

TRUFETTU DELLA ROSSA

"Our spies confirm the Balange will revolt.

They lead a Ligurian lightning bolt.

Spinola's two-hundred troops soon deploy.

They shock all with the tactics they employ."

GHJUDICE DELLA ROSSA

"I made it look as if I do not care.

I am a tired judge with an empty stare.

Yet, four hundred of our troops now arise.

The Commune will effect such a surprise."

LADRU

"I realize my role, but prefer to fight.

I want my home to deploy her sure might.

Spinola is clever with eyes that glare.

The set cold stone looks back if he may dare."

TRUFETTU

"Our host can arrive in less than one day.

While they still taste salt from the sea's spray.

Our rock walls mimic the Spartans at war.

They will be trapped close to the rocky shore."

Thomas Spinola and Several Lesser Counts Lead the Crack Genoese Troops to Feliceto – 1259 CE

COUNT BUONU DI ANTONINU

"We make good time with the judge far away.

Take the best food we want along the way.

We approach a key hidden mountain pass.

Merusaglia falls before the next Mass."

THOMAS SPINOLA, GENOESE GENERAL

"This is a sure bowl with a high ridgeline.

The people offer us fresh bread and wine.

Yet, it reminds me of Alesia's field.

Where the higher Romans made the Gauls yield."

COUNT ORECHIATTA DI CINARCA

"I came to the Balange to start this war.

The path before us is an open door.

We know this new gauntlet of standing stone.

We will then show you we are all alone."

THOMAS SPINOLA

"Keep the vanguard vigilant with sharp eyes.

Let us follow the path of our own spies.

I prefer pikes and sword to open sides.

Caution is the general which today presides."

VIVALDUS MAXIMUS, GENOESE CAPTAIN

"The men are compact ready for battle.

But, ask why do the stones and earth rattle?

How can there be troops there along each side?

Do we march with high flags and hubric pride?"

Ghjudice della Rossa and Trufettu della Rossa Meet with Thomas Spinola, Genoese General, and Vivaldus Maximus, Genoese Captain Before and During the Battle of Feliceto – 1259 CE

GHJUDICE DELLA ROCCA

"The counts' lust led your troops into this vise.

They could mislead you despite being wise.

These brash counts must pay for their wanton lie.

But, your men have homes and need not now die."

THOMAS SPINOLA, GENOESE GENERAL

"We are Templar hard and eager to fight.

You have more men, but we still have more might.

We gave our true word to renounce your role.

We fight not for life, but to keep our soul."

TRUFETTU DELLA ROCCA

"Horns start bloodshed's true path for troops to die.

You can watch the sure goal of the counts' lie.

Greek fire pours down with relentless ease.

We destroy your men however we please."

VIVALDUS MAXIMUS, GENOESE CAPTAIN

"Our skill is no match for a rabid boar.

This is much more slaughter than civil war.

Our men wish they were back on their own ship.

As blood-flesh river rises over each hip."

THOMAS SPINOLA, GENOESE GENERAL

"How could I let this happen to my men?

My troops are caught like young pigs in a pen!

The judge prevails over Genoa's best.

Strike the banners and end this hollow test."

**Thomas Spinola, Genoese general, and Ghjudice della Rocca Reach a Quick Pact
After the Battle of Feliceto Applicable to the Genoese Troops Only – 1259 CE**

GHJUDICE DELLA ROCCA

"Treat each man well as you would your own son.

Give them sweet balm for the honor they won.

We grant them safe passage to their own land.

Those who interfere will die at our hand."

THOMAS SPINOLA, GENOESE GENERAL

"We have lost half of my men and supplies.

We now know the weakness of our allies.

We have respect for a pike and deft hand.

But, Genoa still covets this grand land."

GHJUDICE DELLA ROCCA

"Counts must demur covering what was lost.

They shall repay you and us for our costs.

We support the Commune and village life.

Counts will now build and not further new strife."

TRUFETTU DELLA ROCCA

"The Genoese men are back on their boats.

They have been well fed and given new coats.

Yet, one of their men lost his furloughed life.

Our man cut his throat with his own clan knife."

GHJUDICE DELLA ROCCA

"Bring me he who defied our solemn pledge.

He shall hang all day on a public ledge.

Our win is empty if our word is lost.

We will note this day with this certain cost."

After Ghjudice della Rocca Has Pacified Corsica, He, Massimo, Representative of the Commune. and Consiglio degli Anzani, Pisan Lord, at the Commune in Merusaglia – 1264 CE

CONSIGLIO DEGLI ANZANI, PISAN LORD

"Pisa's hegemony flourishes now.

Village life excels by kids, herd, and plow.

Yet, Ladru and you pledge to our main foe.

Thus, the wide content is saddled with woe."

GHJUDICE DELLA ROCCA

"Richard swore an oath to Saladin too.

And beheaded more Moors when he was through.

Two Genoese strongholds lurk in our land.

We seek balance so your solace can stand."

CONSIGLIO DEGLI ANZANI, PISAN LORD

"We worry our tenure is at its end.

We know how not to break and only bend.

We chose well we put this true judge in charge.

Our success though mirrors our fears so large."

GHJUDICE DELLA ROCCA

"Our fealty to Pisa has not been lost.

We still protect the Commune at all cost.

Trust comes not from words, but from deeds we do.

The counts know that our honor is still true."

MASSIMO, REPRESENTATIVE OF THE COMMUNE

"The judge does secure us with his consent.

Let Bonifaziu stew in dissent.

The Balange did demur with some effect.

But, the people prevail showing their respect."

Ghjudice della Rocca and Trufettu della Rocca Meet a La Donna Signadore in the Aitone Forest – 1264 CE

LA DONNA SIGNADORE

"Your eyes are shot even when they are not.

Danger is a balm when flesh starts to rot.

Do not fall for the elusive boar's cry.

Stay home or you will cast how you will die!"

TRUFETTU

"A boar menaces Morgana's small tract.

We must help to keep our honor intact.

We need only watch for tusks and green eyes.

Unlike a count, a boar's wants never lies."

LA DONNA SIGNADORE

"You do not know how much you speak is true.

Yet, you deny the harm in front of you.

The eyes to fear may not be the ones you think.

Fate occurs more often followed by drink."

GHJUDICE DELLA ROCCA

"How can a judge ignore a woman's plight?

Does not my honor command me to fight?

I will find the counts and bring them to bay.

But, I must address pain in my own way."

LA DONNA SIGNADORE

"Hubris never has honor or foresight.

A boar is not the thing to fear this night.

The powers of pure darkness are at play.

I implore a judge to caution and stay."

Ghjudice della Rocca is Injured Chasing the Boar at the Home of Morganna Where They are Joined by Trufettu and in the Aitone Forest – 1264 CE

MORGANNA (TO HERSELF)

"The judge does not see the trap I have made.

He comes to hunt a rogue boar in the shade.

The tool of his death will be made tonight.

Let me go outside full of fear and fright."

LADRU DELLA ROCCA

"We were on patrol when we heard your call.

Your fear turns your sheer veil into a pall.

Go to your bed this troubled, frenzied night.

Sleep will be the cure for your overt fright."

MORGANNA

"Do not delay, as the boar was just here.

That is the sole source of this present fear.

You cannot wait for the judge to arrive.

Your sloth will help the boar just to survive."

LADRU DELLA ROCCA

"Trufettu's host joins us to start the race.

The boar cannot outrun our pensive pace.

He knows the terrain better than we do.

He challenges us before we may be through."

GHJUDICE DELLA ROCCA (FOLLOWING ALONE)

"I will join my true brothers when I may.

Let us quickly get you inside to stay.

Why did you withdraw from my tired sight?

This delay just forestalls the old boar's plight."

MORGANNA

"I would have been Brutus if I were old.

My knife digs deep spilling your blood so bold.

I will call your brothers back tonight.

Help! Help! The boar came from beyond his sight."

LADRU DELLA ROCCA (RETURNING WHEN CALLED)

"We should have kept him close within our sight.

He bleeds too much to move him from this site.

Where is the boar that could cause so much strife?

Whose tusk is sharp cutting him like a knife."

MORGANNA

"My home is plain, but holds such herbal cures.

My down bed receives while his hope endures.

I want to help him for the real risk he took.

Let him lay waiting for the meal I cook."

TRUFETTU DELLA ROCCA

"We will find that vile boar that maimed him so.

We will chase him with piercing pike and bow.

Let the maquis fuel your true healer's art.

We should leave you alone and let you start."

MORGANNA

"Do not be skeptical or fear too much!

My mortar and pestle mimic my touch.

Return in three days to find him all well.

You will have much more than a tale to tell."

GHJUDICE DELLA ROCCA

"My pain laughs at the purpose of this drink.

We intertwine at the blank boundless brink.

Two serpents as one with no start or end.

Hermes' staff fractures the light it may bend."

MORGANNA

"Does a hero sleep in my own warm bed?

Cyrene and Volpe would prefer you dead.

They and Dido lost seeking their revenge.

But, the child we made will live to avenge."

DEBULE

"Mistress, an old woman knocks at the door.

She acts as if she has been here before.

Here are your robes and braids for your hair.

I will store your caduceus with care."

MORGANNA

"My task is all done, as you arrive too late.

You will not be able to change his fate.

He will lose because of his own pure pride.

But, also because my sharp knife in his side."

LA DONNA SIGNADORE

"Your hubris exceeds his and made you blind.

This is a lesson he needed to find.

Your son, Salnese, may lead to his demise.

He now returns home cleverer and wiser."

Lucca and Mateu, the Descendent Corsican Templars, Observe the Status of the Near World with Ghjudice della Rocca in Olmeto Before They Head to Loretu to Meet with Count Ghjuvannellu Who Has Supported Ghjudice della Rocca and His Brothers and Pisa – 1267 CE

LUCCA, DESCENDENT CORSICAN TEMPLAR

"The Pisan peace expands with a monk's zeal.

The tangible benefits are very real.

We and the Commune reject kings and Pope.

You as judge provide the people with hope."

MATEU, DESCENDENT CORSICAN TEMPLAR

"Aachen, Paris and London vie for land.

Kings maneuver puppet counts to command.

Popes and princes will be the newest Moors.

Keep peace with the counts to preserve our shores."

LUCCA, DESCENDENT CORSICAN TEMPLAR

"Counts are like diffuse water on the land.

Left alone they play a capricious hand.

But give them an aqueduct's course to run.

They bring the hope and light of the Sun."

MATEU DESCENDENT CORSICAN COUNT

"You serve Thomas' and the Saint King's measure.

Guidance yields the common good as treasure.

Yet, the sea churns with ships seeking greed.

They do not care of the people to feed."

GHJUDICE DELLA ROCCA

"We now go to Loretu to seize the day.

We secure the counts that support our way.

Let the red cross show the favor we earn.

Our pacts will show the judgment we may learn."

Pascal Paul Piazza

Victor Doria, Genoese General, Tries to Subvert the Fealty of Count Ghjuvannellu and Count Basie in Loretu – 1267 CE

VICTOR DORIA, GENOESE GENERAL

"Why do you counts just hunt, whore, bunker and hide?

You have shown no pride since Arrigo died.

Genoa shall soon retake full control.

Your men should attack with speed on patrol."

COUNT BASIE

"We pledge to Pisa and thus keep our home.

We need not fight like Aachen battles Rome.

We have our castle, our land and good trade.

These are the gains of a safe pact well made."

COUNT GHJUVANNELLU

"Your words bellow forth nothing but hot air.

Your crack troops lost and left the Balange bare.

The judge respects while you seem not to care.

We thrive in a land both fruitful and fair."

VICTOR DORIA, GENOESE GENERAL

"We embark on a crusading campaign.

Aiacciu first will fall in Spring rain.

Then Calvi grows into our entrepot.

Troops flow like torrents as our rule will grow."

COUNT GHJUVANNELLU

"Leave now, as we have pulsing plans to make.

We will start a war though its cause is fake.

It will surpass Ghilbertine versus Guelph.

We forsake honor for the vice of wealth."

Ghjudice della Rocca Meets with Longstanding Friend, Count Ghjuvannellu, While Their Men Hunt and Engage in Combat Games and Fun – 1267 CE

COUNT GHJUVANNELLU

"Why hunt with us when we hunted your blood?

Why do you help us when our rivers flood?

You know we suffer from Ligurian lust.

Yet, you treat us with such a special trust."

GHJUDICE DELLA ROCCA

"My cousins murdered my father, not you.

I am judge for all and not just a few.

I know you want the counts' rights back in full.

Your people starve if I kill their own bull."

COUNT GHJUVANNELLU

"You come to keep the peace that is in place.

I sense though that we run in some new race.

Let our men and women enjoy the most.

I have many that are fresh from the coast."

GHJUDICE DELLA ROCCA

"Why was that young dog thrown at my man's face?

Is that a custom from some foreign place?

My captain throws it back and it hits you.

Is that what we were now supposed to do?"

COUNT GHJUVANNELLU

"This is an insult of the highest rank.

You dishonor me with this petty prank.

Withdraw all your men now with such disgrace.

We are now mortal foes in time and space!"

**The Feud Continues Unabated for Over Thirty Years While Ghjudice della Rocca Also Fights
Luchetto Doria, Genoese General, Over an Enlarged Port of Calvi, Incursions in the Balange,
and Control of Aiacciu and Southwest Corsica. Ghjudice della Rocca, Lucca and Mateu, Descendent
Corsican Templars, Jacopo Orsini, Duke of Pisa, Oberto, Papal Legate and Luchetto Doria, Genoese
General, Attend a Truce Assembly at Monticellu Beginning with
a Summary from the Corsican Templars and Witnessing the End of the Pisan Peace – 1299 CE**

LUCCA, DESCENDENT CORSICAN TEMPLAR

"The Saint King died on the last crusade made.

Prince Edward did not give the Saint King aid.

He went East making pacts both day and night.

Now, Urban's dream has died without a fight."

MATEU, DESCENDENT CORSICAN TEMPLAR

"Aragon held strong and retook much land.

We tried to hold Acre with one last stand.

The West sent no counts against Baibar's host.

They fought themselves when we needed them most."

LUCCA, DESCENDENT CORSICAN TEMPLAR

"Edward now invests Scotland, France and Wales.

Pisa just fell to Genoa's black sails.

Germans and Rome contest the Papal States.

The French Kings add to their regal estates."

MATEU, DESCENDENT CORSICAN TEMPLAR

"We relocate where we best can be free.

We lodge in the South and across the Sea.

Our commanderies support freedom's cause.

We buffer against capricious laws."

LUCCA, DESCENDENT CORSICAN TEMPLAR

"Kings and Popes owe us more money each day.

We and you impede their bald power play.

There will be a target on each of our backs.

Look for royal rule and secret attacks."

JACAPO ORSINI, DUKE OF PISA

"Eleven years ago our force ended.

All oaths to us were void and suspended.

You fought Luchetto's men without our aid.

We hereby cede the isle by treaty made."

LUCHETTO DORIA, GENOESE GENERAL

"I accept that Pisa now cedes this place.

Our flags signal we did win this long race.

Our ban on the judge goes into effect.

It extends to his allies we suspect."

OBERTO, PAPAL LEGATE

"We welcome your bold zeal to find peace here.

But, that you will now rule is not clear.

In Rome, the Pope invested a new king.

He gave all land to James with a new ring."

GHJUDICE DELLA ROCCA

"We talk this day under a flag of truce.

My vigor vests like a strong oak or spruce.

I will welcome when Luchetto goes home.

And this silky peacock returns to Rome."

TRUFETTU DELLA ROCCA

"Our troops will soon surround all men they meet.
Our women lust to sink Genoa's fleet.
The Commune fights like no boar you have seen.
You will have to drink your bile from your spleen."

GHJUDICE DELLA ROCCA

"I speak directly to a troubled foe.
Why do you ignore your men's pain and woe?
In the past decade what deeds have been done?
You achieve less than the lesser counts have won!"

LADRU DELLA ROCCA

"A fake vendetta started a new war.
Your stooge counts died on chosen stone and shore.
New counts arise, but will fail to survive.
The judge and his brothers remain alive."

TRUFETTU DELLA ROCCA

"The request to save Calvi was your fuse.
To bring peace to battling counts was a ruse.
Genoa made Calvi a major port.
We took it before you could build a fort."

GHJUDICE DELLA ROCCA

"We released Calvi after just two years.
During which we employed defensive weirs.
We welcome if you have your troops muster.
They will fall by one or as they cluster."

LADRU DELLA ROCCA

"Your settlers fell to the Anjou's axe that falls.
They were caught within Aiacciu's walls.
Promises of freedom fell of death's ears.
Genoa's gambit lost in two short years."

LUCHETTO DORIA

"My men are not those who came before me.

They will not give up as you will soon see.

Bulgar, Byzantine, and Berber have lost.

Moor, Arab, and Turk know the final cost."

GHJUDICE DELLA ROCCA

"Yet, you only rule some towns on the coast.

You have no conquests beyond there to boast.

You may burn a castle or raze a field.

Each village is strong refusing to yield."

LUCHETTO DORIA

"My best troops are a nut you cannot crack.

That is why you seek truce flat on your back.

You hesitate and how your true fears.

You cannot stand to fight for the next years."

GHJUDICE DELLA ROCCA

"You and I have fought a protracted fight.

Leaving too many widows grieve at night.

Yes, I sought peace to stop bloodshed so raw.

I had hoped you too saw that what I saw."

LUCHETTO DORIA

"Hector now takes the sole command to win.

You will soon see Hercules' mortal twin.

There will be such tales of my wars to be.

The annals of war will know only me."

Ghjudice della Rocca and Luchetto Doria, Genoese General, Meet at the Spring of Olmeto – 1304 CE

GHJUDICE DELLA ROCCA

"You journey long to my old springs to drink.

Do you find these waters help you think?

In six years your men still fail, lose and bleed.

The land eludes you even with your deed."

LUCHETTO DORIA, GENOESE GENERAL

"How can you survive without Pisa's aid?

We have mercenaries who are well paid.

We thought you would adopt Fabian's tack.

Yet, you pursued Scipio's full attack."

GHJUDICE DELLA ROCCA

"My troops are not conscripts or seeking pay.

They rally more win or lose each new day.

You will never know the island's true path.

Our homes are much more secure with your wrath."

LUCHETTO DORIA, GENOESE GENERAL

"It took many years for Pisa to fall.

Six years lost is next to nothing at all.

Twenty thousand more men can soon be found.

We will not stop until we control all ground."

GHJUDICE DELLA ROCCA

"We will fight even if it is just me.

I will throw your black banners in the Sea.

I offer you quarter without any fee,

If we fight, we will surely remain free."

Luchetto Doria, Genoese General, and Oberto Dorian, Captain of a Genoese Guard, Decide a Major Attack on Aleria to Try to Break the Support for Ghjudice della Rocca – 1305 CE

LUCHETTO DORIA, GENOESE GENERAL

"The judge believes Aleria is secure.

That false belief will be our next sure lure.

When he learns that the port will soon be lost.

He will come east quickly at all cost."

OBERTO DORIA, CAPTAIN OF A GENOESE GUARD

"We have set up strong traps on each known route.

Our strongest troops deploy without doubt.

The carnage will rival Cannae's worst day.

The judge will soon have little left to say."

LUCHETTO DORIA, GENOESE GENERAL

"The battles are joined with flares in the air.

Let our flags rustle in the wind with flair.

I need news of our win before the day ends.

We need the joy only victory sends."

OBERTO DORIA, CAPTAIN OF THE GENOESE GUARD

"We have suffered a serious defeat.

All our troops run in a massive retreat.

The judge found paths that we did not know.

Dead bodies detail the plain row by row."

LUCHETTO DORIA, GENOESE GENERAL

"Let us now sue for peace if we still can.

Right now, we must not lose another man.

Except I must do what honor entails.

Please tell mother these very sad details."

Pascal Paul Piazza

Count Guglielmo della Petrallarretta Unsuccessfully Seeks Revenge against Ghjudice della Rocca for the Treatment of His Father, Count Ugo della Petrallarretta, When Ghjudice della Rocca is Betrayed by His Bastard Son, Salnese della Rocca, and Lupu d'Ornanu in Olmeto – 1306 CE

GHJUDICE DELLA ROCCA

"Ugo's son is no stressful match for me.

I am ninety years old and my home is free.

My friend Lupu brings me a young woman.

She is modest with black hair and dark tan."

DESERETTE

"You must leave now, as this is a sure trap.

I came here today to give you this map.

My mother said you were sharp as an owl.

Leave through the window using your old trowel."

SALNESE DELLA ROCCA

"Where is the old judge you were to seduce?

What vile ploy did you and he deduce?

I will post your head in the village square.

You will pay for your deceit as you dare."

GHJUDICE DELLA ROCCA

"I cannot leave her without any aid.

I will stand by the mistakes that I made.

Come close my son and feel now my own strife.

As a Corsican with my mortal knife."

LUPU D'ORNANU

"The judge is bound now for the Genoese rain.

He will spend his life in jail and in pain.

We will kill his brothers when all is said.

Will they guard their homes when he is dead?"

Deserette Meets with Ghjudice della Rocca in His Jail Cell in Genoa – 1307 CE

GHJUDICE DELLA ROCCA

"How did you get past the guards at the door?

I am a sad sight laid prone on the floor.

I am hardly the judge the people need.

I have abandoned them while they bleed."

DESERETTE

"I could seduce the young guards as I please.

I have a cart so we can leave with ease.

You were betrayed by your friend and your son.

There is still a great battle to be won."

GHJUDICE DELLA ROCCA

"My pride and hubris were my biggest foes.

I am too old to withstand all my woes.

The terraces do not need me to be free.

They need no more grave despair caused by me."

DESERETTE

"You were a beacon beaming from the hill.

As a child, I was taught of your skill.

You plot the path for patriots to be.

Arthur's purest knight is who I now see."

GHJUDICE DELLA ROCCA

"You breathe a hot fire in my cold heart.

But, I just cannot perform my old part.

I had lost my soul and soon I must die.

Tell the truth about me and not a lie."

King Phillip IV of France and Pope Clement V Meet in Paris – 1307 CE

PHILIP IV THE FAIR, KING OF FRANCE

"I made peace with Edward when he did ask.

I now join him in this most royal task.

We will scatter freeholds like shards of pots.

As Edward did with the Welsh and the Scots."

POPE CLEMENT V

"You were free to end aid to Wallace's ploy.

Now it is time for your troops to deploy.

Send the heretic Templars to their grave.

There is nothing but their riches to save."

PHILLIP IV THE FAIR, KING OF FRANCE

"On Friday the thirteenth arrests will start.

Each Templar answers for his role or part.

Their lands are forfeit with riches release.

Our coffers increase while our debts decrease."

POPE CLEMENT V

"It is time to kill the judge still in jail.

His ongoing life just adds to his tale.

Find some Doria to cut off his head.

The Commune will fail once he is soon dead."

JOAN OF NAVARRE, QUEEN OF FRANCE

"You seek to destroy two models for me.

They made it known what true freedom could be.

You seek to cancel the debt in your burse.

Yet, you two invoke your own deadly curse."

Lucca and Mateu, the Descendent Corsican Templars Like Most of the Templars, Left Before being Arrested and Arrive at Merusaglia with News of the Judge – 1307 CE

LUCCA, DESCENDENT CORSICAN TEMPLAR

"Genoese news states that the judge did die.

He was taken by one practiced to lie.

His brothers were drawn, cut, and split in two.

Two hundred years of Pisan peace dies too."

MATEU, DESCENDENT CORSICAN TEMPLAR

"Phillip today revealed his iron hand.

He sought to find each Templar in his land.

We were mainly gone with no riches found.

Save our Master who was roughly bound."

LUCCA, DESCENDENT CORSICAN TEMPLAR

"Our wealth of the East is now freedom's seed.

From this isle to Lisbon it serves one need.

It will arise with no flag or fanfare.

A red or Lorraine cross shows it is there."

MATEU, DESCENDENT CORSICAN TEMPLAR

"Genoa finds it worse to rule than fight.

Freemen will arise to fight Genoa's might.

Pisa's peace passes to patriots bold.

Therein is an epic poem new and old."

LUCCA, DESCENDENT CORSICAN TEMPLAR

"Interludes end on a foundation laid.

Freedom asks such a high price to be paid.

The isle's pure traits will be strewn far and near.

They will connect her heirs to this land so dear."

TIME TABLE

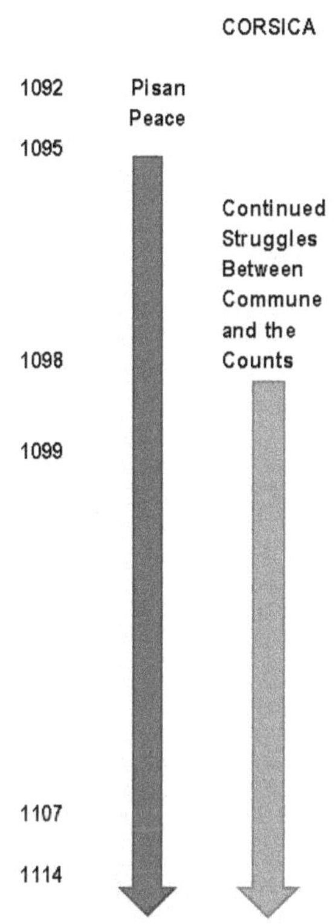

	CORSICA	EUROPE RELATED TO CORSICA	CRUSADES RELATED TO CORSICA
1092	Pisan Peace		
1095			Pope Urban II calls for the First Crusade Major Crusading armies leave form Southwest France and travel the trade routes involving Corsica
	Continued Struggles Between Commune and the Counts	Corsica is part of the continuing counterpoise in the Italian city states, parts of German states, and England for assemblies or communes as balance to kings or counts	Pisa joins the Crusading armies
1098			County of Edessa and Principality of Antioch founded
1099		Rest of western Europe saw increase in decentralization, the rise of feudalism and control by counts from castles and manors, and decreased focus on the public good	Jerusalem falls. Godfrey named Advocate
			Daimbert of Pisa invests Latakia Daimbert to Pisa named Patriarch of Jerusalem
			Kingdom of Jerusalem founded with King Baldwin I
			Daimbert of Pisa and Bohemond vie with King Baldwin I and meet Pope
1107			Daimbert of Pisa dies
1114			Catalan Crusade to the Balearic Islands Corsica part of trade zone with Narbo and Catalonia

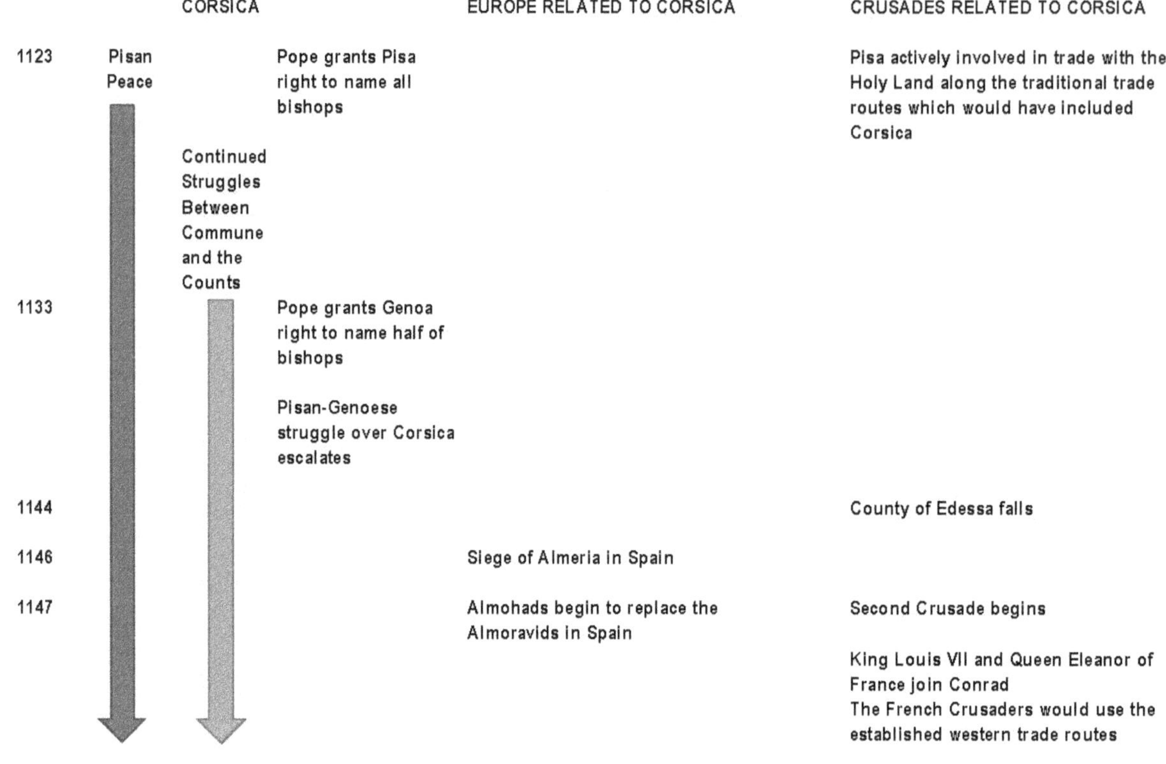
CORSICA
EUROPE RELATED TO CORSICA
CRUSADES RELATED TO CORSICA
1123
Pisan
Peace
Pope grants Pisa
right to name all
bishops
Pisa actively involved in trade with the
Holy Land along the traditional trade
routes which would have included
Corsica
Continued
Struggles
Between
Commune
and the
Counts
1133
Pope grants Genoa
right to name half of
bishops
Pisan-Genoese
struggle over Corsica
escalates
1144
County of Edessa falls
1146
Siege of Almeria in Spain
1147
Almohads begin to replace the
Almoravids in Spain
Second Crusade begins
King Louis VII and Queen Eleanor of
France join Conrad
The French Crusaders would use the
established western trade routes
2

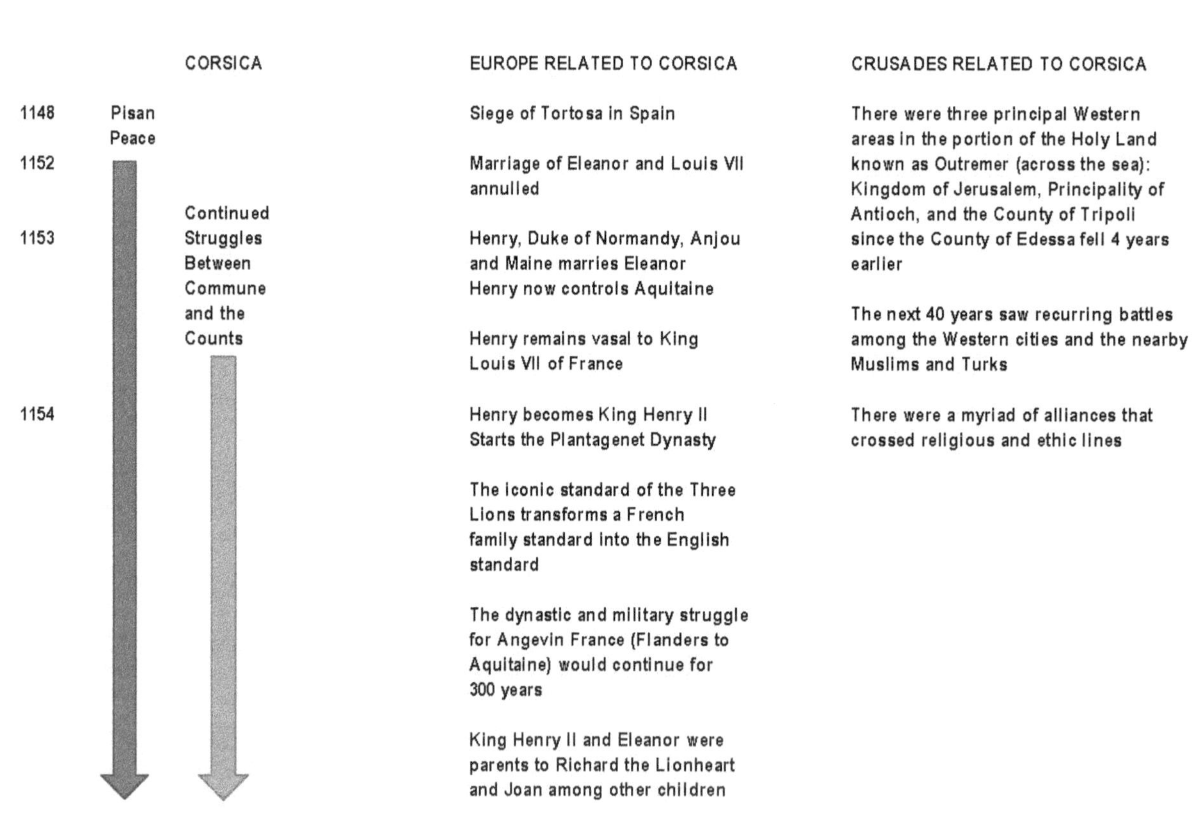
CORSICA
EUROPE RELATED TO CORSICA
CRUSADES RELATED TO CORSICA
1148
Pisan
Peace
Siege of Tortosa in Spain
There were three principal Western
areas in the portion of the Holy Land
1152
Marriage of Eleanor and Louis VII
annulled
known as Outremer (across the sea):
Kingdom of Jerusalem, Principality of
Antioch, and the County of Tripoli
Continued
1153
Struggles
Between
Commune
and the
Counts
Henry, Duke of Normandy, Anjou
and Maine marries Eleanor
Henry now controls Aquitaine
since the County of Edessa fell 4 years
earlier
The next 40 years saw recurring battles
Henry remains vasal to King
Louis VII of France
among the Western cities and the nearby
Muslims and Turks
1154
Henry becomes King Henry II
Starts the Plantagenet Dynasty
There were a myriad of alliances that
crossed religious and ethic lines
The iconic standard of the Three
Lions transforms a French
family standard into the English
standard
The dynastic and military struggle
for Angevin France (Flanders to
Aquitaine) would continue for
300 years
King Henry II and Eleanor were
parents to Richard the Lionheart
and Joan among other children
3

CORSICA
EUROPE RELATED TO CORSICA
CRUSADES RELATED TO CORSICA

1168
Pisan Peace

1174

1177
Continued Struggles Between Commune and the Counts

1179
1180

1186

1187

1188

Richard the Lionheart banishes his vassals, Guy and Geoffrey de Lusignan from Poitiers

Joan, age 11, weds King William II of Sicily

King Phillip II of France succeeds King Louis VII

King Henry II takes Cross at Tours
He would never travel east. Rather, he would defeat Crusader heroes, Robert of Normandy and Robert of Flanders.

King Phillip II takes Cross at St Denis

Muslim resurgence under Nuredin

Saladin consolidates power in Egypt

Guy de Lusignan arrives in the Holy Land

Guy de Lusignan becomes King of Jerusalem

Saladin defeats King Guy de Lusignan at the Horns of Hattin

Saladin decapitates the Templars and Reynald de Chatillon, but saves King Guy de Lusignan
The Templars almost extinguished

Richard the Lionheart takes the cross

Saladin releases King Guy de Lusignan

King Guy de Lusignan begins 3 year battle with Conrad de Monferrat

Guy de Lusignan and Geoffrey de Lusignan begin 4 year siege of Acre

CORSICA
EUROPE RELATED TO CORSICA
CRUSADES RELATED TO CORSICA

1188-1190
Pisan Peace

Continued Struggles Between Commune and the Counts

King Henry II and King Phillip II fight over the Angevin lands, thus delaying the start of any Crusade

Richard the Lionheart puts down revolt in Aquitaine and Toulouse

Richard the Lionheart allies with King Phillip II against King Henry II

King Henry cedes crown to King Richard the Lionheart

King Richard the Lionheart battles with King Phillip II over the Angevin lands

The Dowager Queen Joan of Sicily put under house arrest by King Tancred of Sicily

The Saladin tax or tithe has been in effect since after Hattin

King Richard is well funded with 200 ships

King Phillip II has smaller, but efficient army

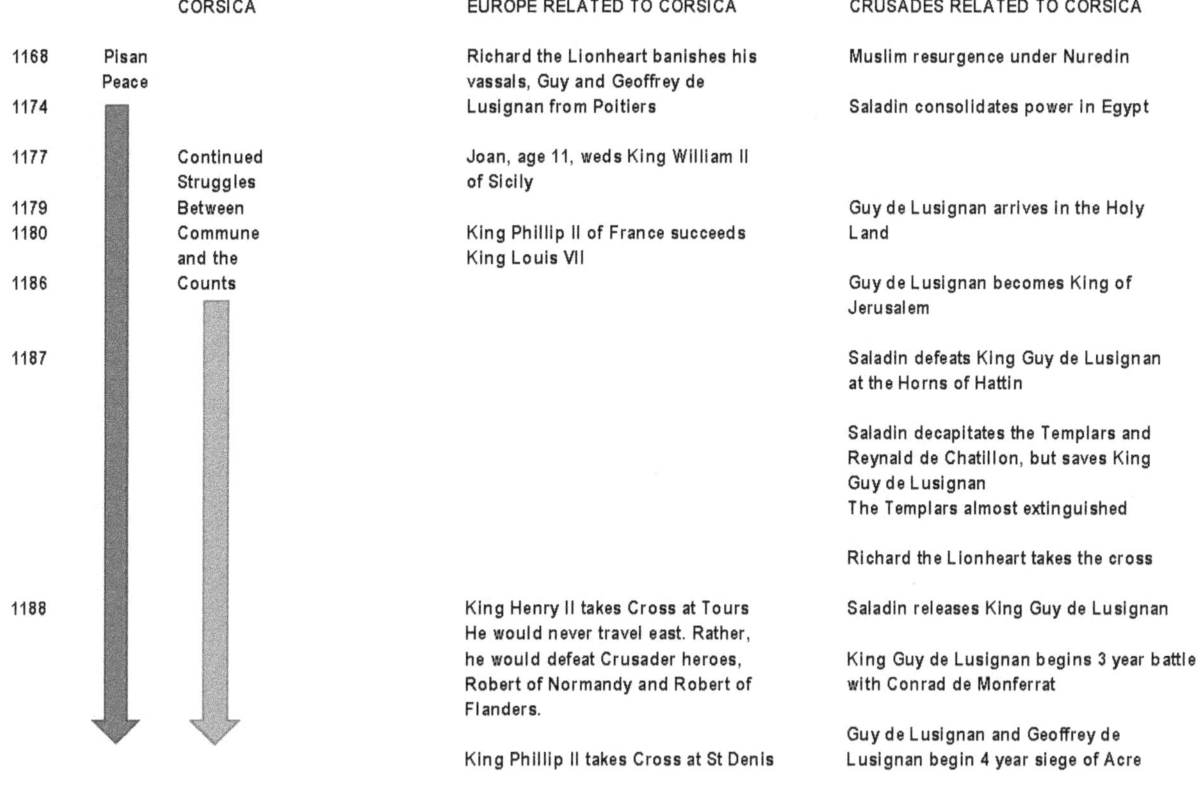

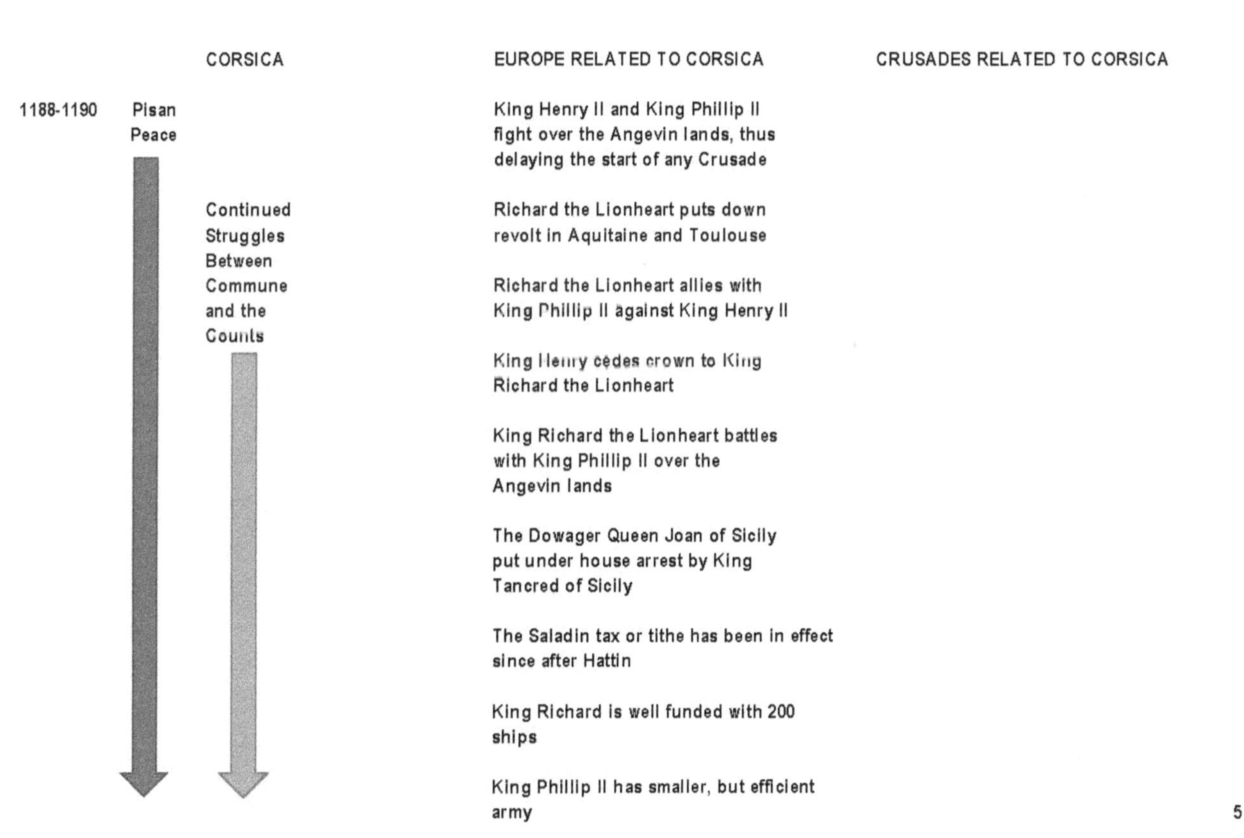

5

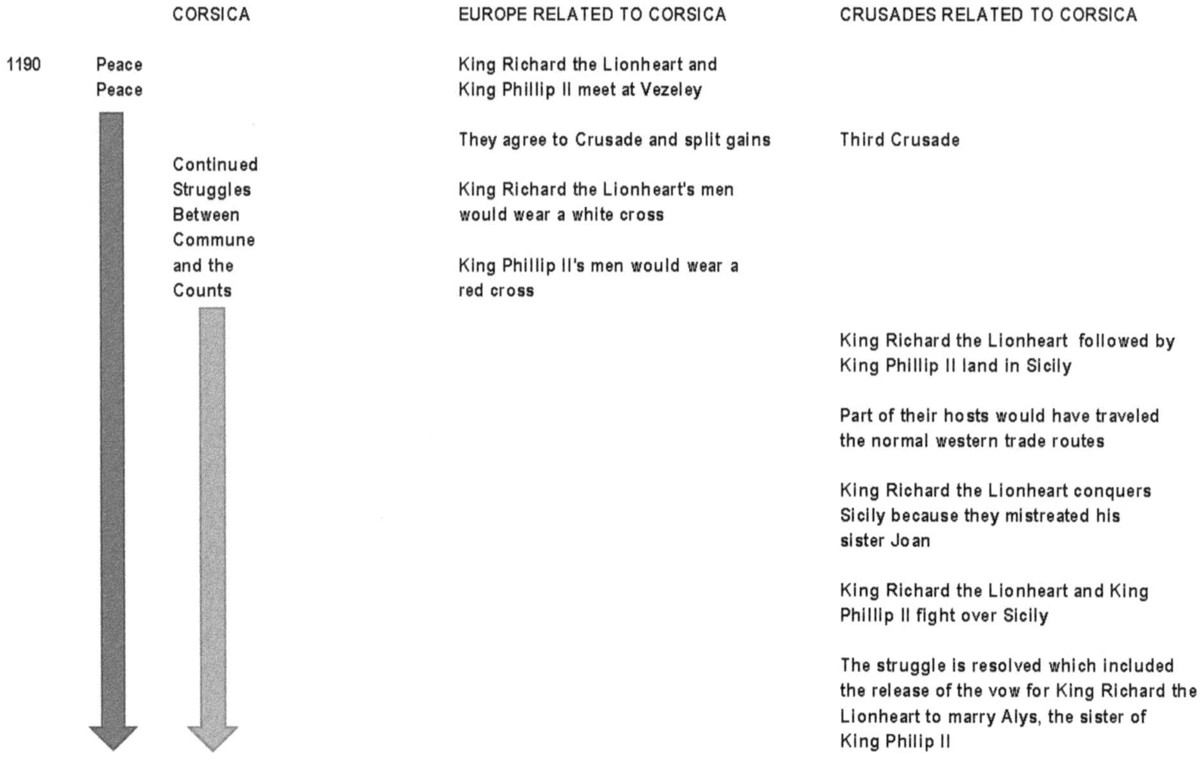
CORSICA
EUROPE RELATED TO CORSICA
CRUSADES RELATED TO CORSICA
1190
Peace
Peace
Continued
Struggles
Between
Commune
and the
Counts
King Richard the Lionheart and
King Phillip II meet at Vezeley
They agree to Crusade and split gains
King Richard the Lionheart's men
would wear a white cross
King Phillip II's men would wear a
red cross
Third Crusade
King Richard the Lionheart followed by
King Phillip II land in Sicily
Part of their hosts would have traveled
the normal western trade routes
King Richard the Lionheart conquers
Sicily because they mistreated his
sister Joan
King Richard the Lionheart and King
Phillip II fight over Sicily
The struggle is resolved which included
the release of the vow for King Richard the
Lionheart to marry Alys, the sister of
King Philip II
6

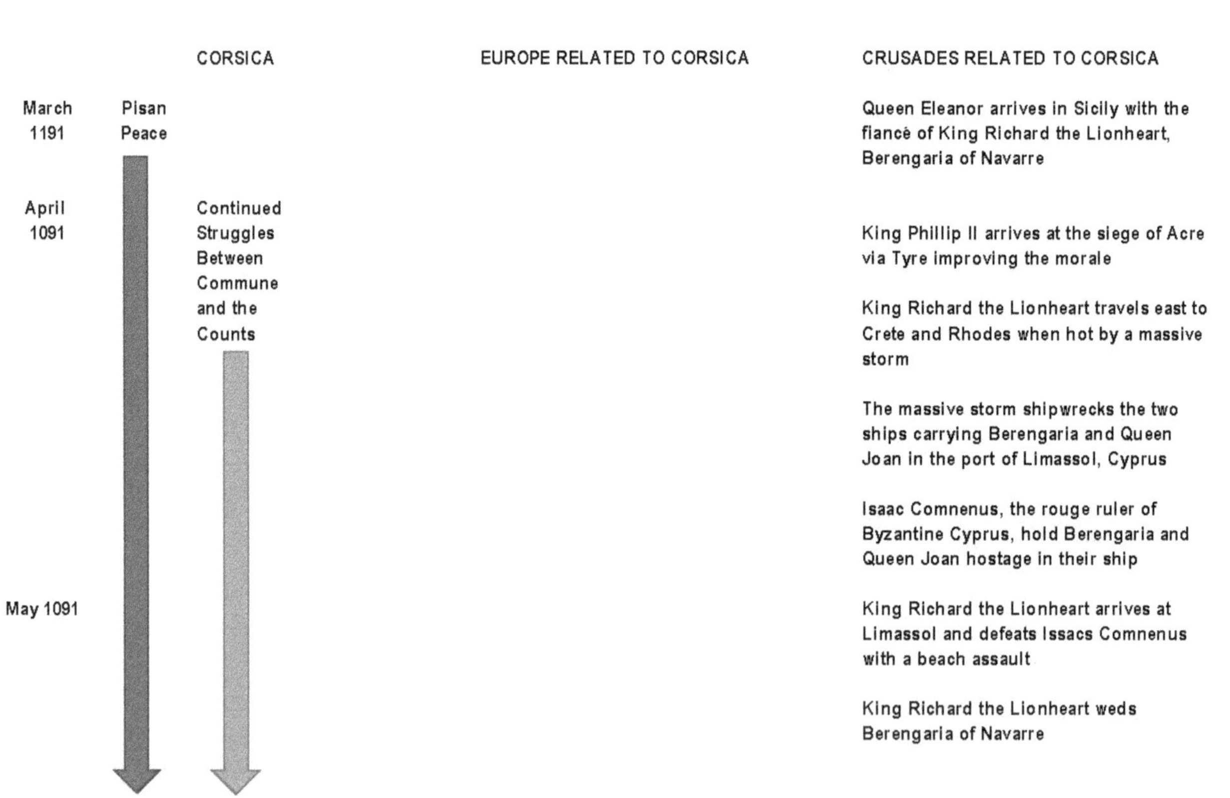
CORSICA
EUROPE RELATED TO CORSICA
CRUSADES RELATED TO CORSICA
March
1191
Pisan
Peace
April
1091
Continued
Struggles
Between
Commune
and the
Counts
May 1091
Queen Eleanor arrives in Sicily with the
fiancè of King Richard the Lionheart,
Berengaria of Navarre
King Phillip II arrives at the siege of Acre
via Tyre improving the morale
King Richard the Lionheart travels east to
Crete and Rhodes when hot by a massive
storm
The massive storm shipwrecks the two
ships carrying Berengaria and Queen
Joan in the port of Limassol, Cyprus
Isaac Comnenus, the rouge ruler of
Byzantine Cyprus, hold Berengaria and
Queen Joan hostage in their ship
King Richard the Lionheart arrives at
Limassol and defeats Issacs Comnenus
with a beach assault
King Richard the Lionheart weds
Berengaria of Navarre
7

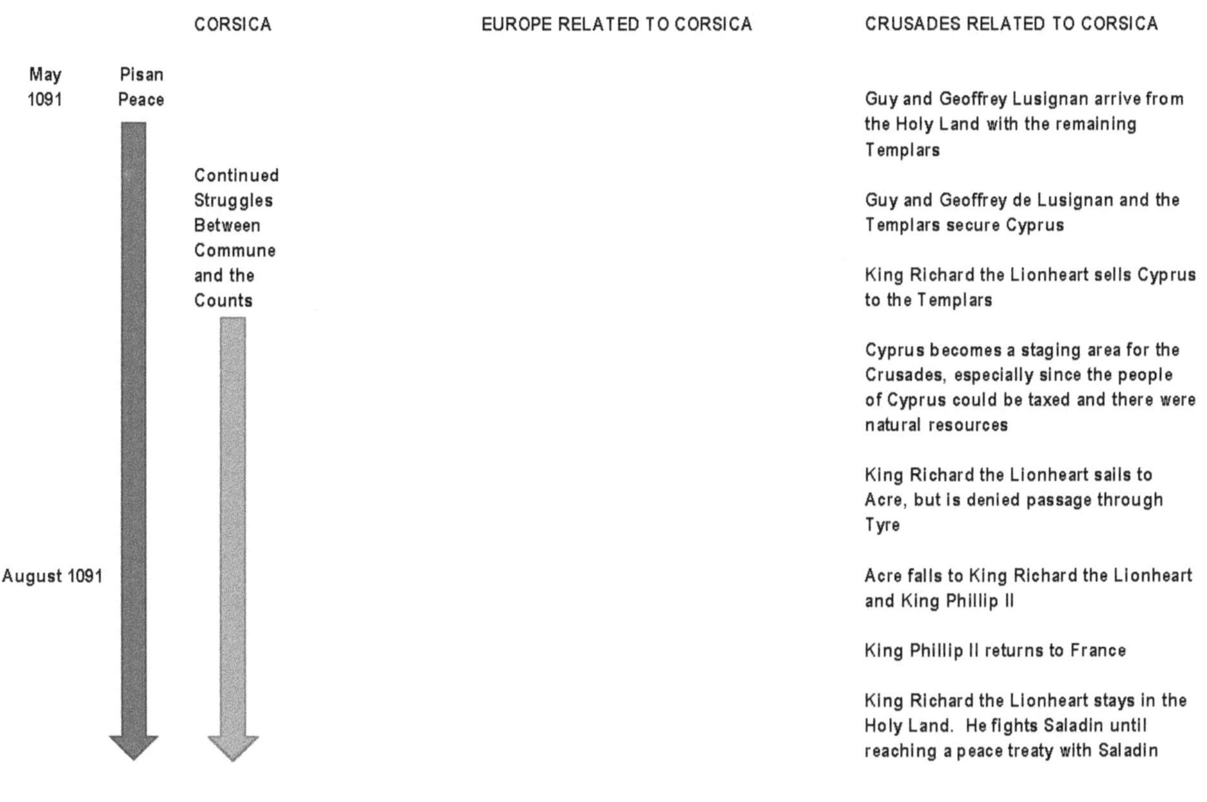
CORSICA

EUROPE RELATED TO CORSICA

CRUSADES RELATED TO CORSICA

May 1091

Pisan Peace

Continued Struggles Between Commune and the Counts

Guy and Geoffrey Lusignan arrive from the Holy Land with the remaining Templars

Guy and Geoffrey de Lusignan and the Templars secure Cyprus

King Richard the Lionheart sells Cyprus to the Templars

Cyprus becomes a staging area for the Crusades, especially since the people of Cyprus could be taxed and there were natural resources

King Richard the Lionheart sails to Acre, but is denied passage through Tyre

August 1091

Acre falls to King Richard the Lionheart and King Phillip II

King Phillip II returns to France

King Richard the Lionheart stays in the Holy Land. He fights Saladin until reaching a peace treaty with Saladin

8

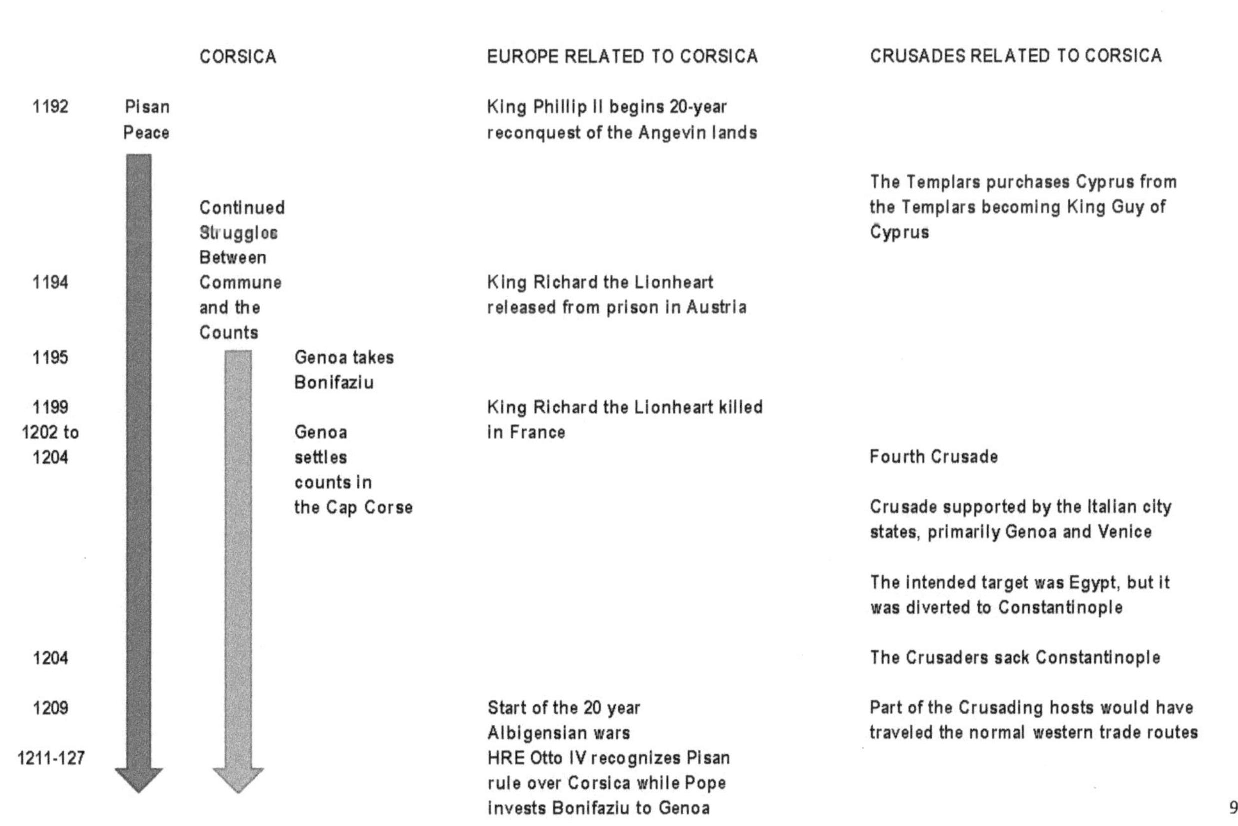
CORSICA

EUROPE RELATED TO CORSICA

CRUSADES RELATED TO CORSICA

1192

Pisan Peace

King Phillip II begins 20-year reconquest of the Angevin lands

The Templars purchases Cyprus from the Templars becoming King Guy of Cyprus

Continued Struggles Between Commune and the Counts

1194

King Richard the Lionheart released from prison in Austria

1195

Genoa takes Bonifaziu

1199

King Richard the Lionheart killed in France

1202 to 1204

Genoa settles counts in the Cap Corse

Fourth Crusade

Crusade supported by the Italian city states, primarily Genoa and Venice

The intended target was Egypt, but it was diverted to Constantinople

1204

The Crusaders sack Constantinople

1209

Start of the 20 year Albigensian wars

Part of the Crusading hosts would have traveled the normal western trade routes

1211-127

HRE Otto IV recognizes Pisan rule over Corsica while Pope invests Bonifaziu to Genoa

9

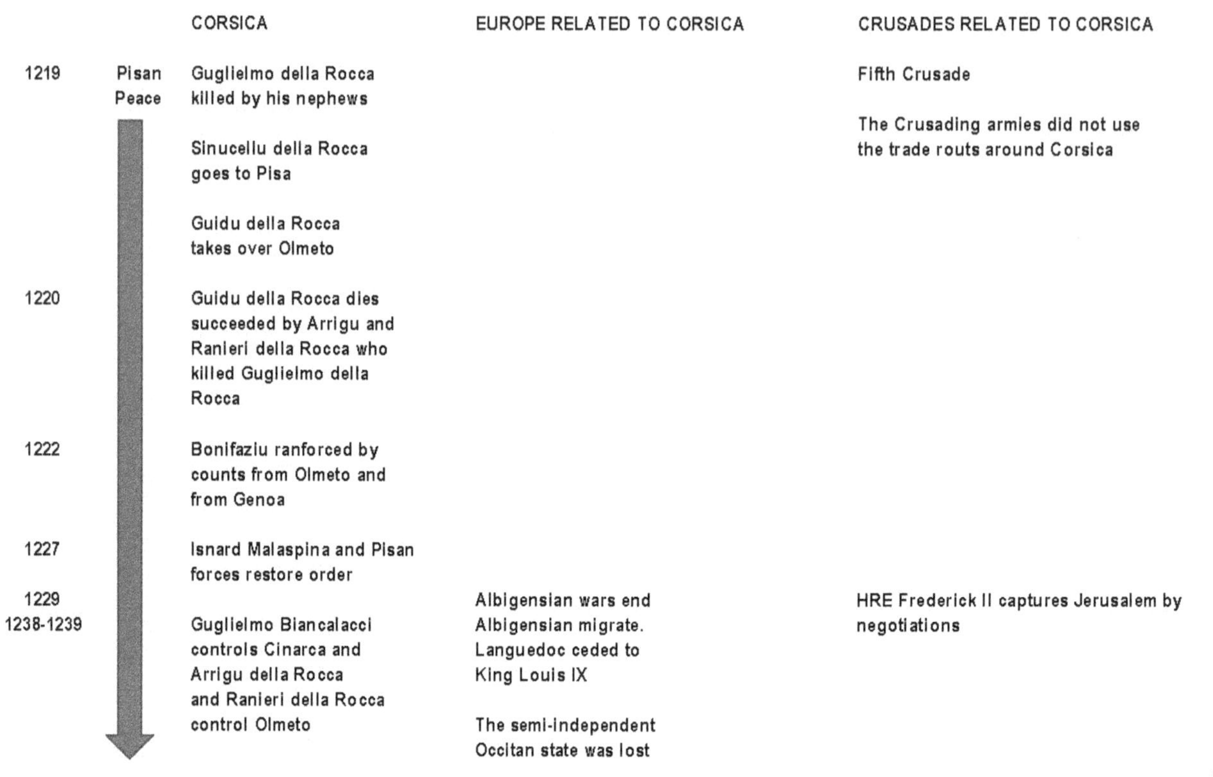

		CORSICA	EUROPE RELATED TO CORSICA	CRUSADES RELATED TO CORSICA
1219	Pisan Peace	Guglielmo della Rocca killed by his nephews		Fifth Crusade
		Sinucellu della Rocca goes to Pisa		The Crusading armies did not use the trade routs around Corsica
		Guidu della Rocca takes over Olmeto		
1220		Guidu della Rocca dies succeeded by Arrigu and Ranieri della Rocca who killed Guglielmo della Rocca		
1222		Bonifaziu ranforced by counts from Olmeto and from Genoa		
1227		Isnard Malaspina and Pisan forces restore order		
1229			Albigensian wars end	HRE Frederick II captures Jerusalem by negotiations
1238-1239		Guglielmo Biancalacci controls Cinarca and Arrigu della Rocca and Ranieri della Rocca control Olmeto	Albigensian migrate. Languedoc ceded to King Louis IX The semi-independent Occitan state was lost	

10

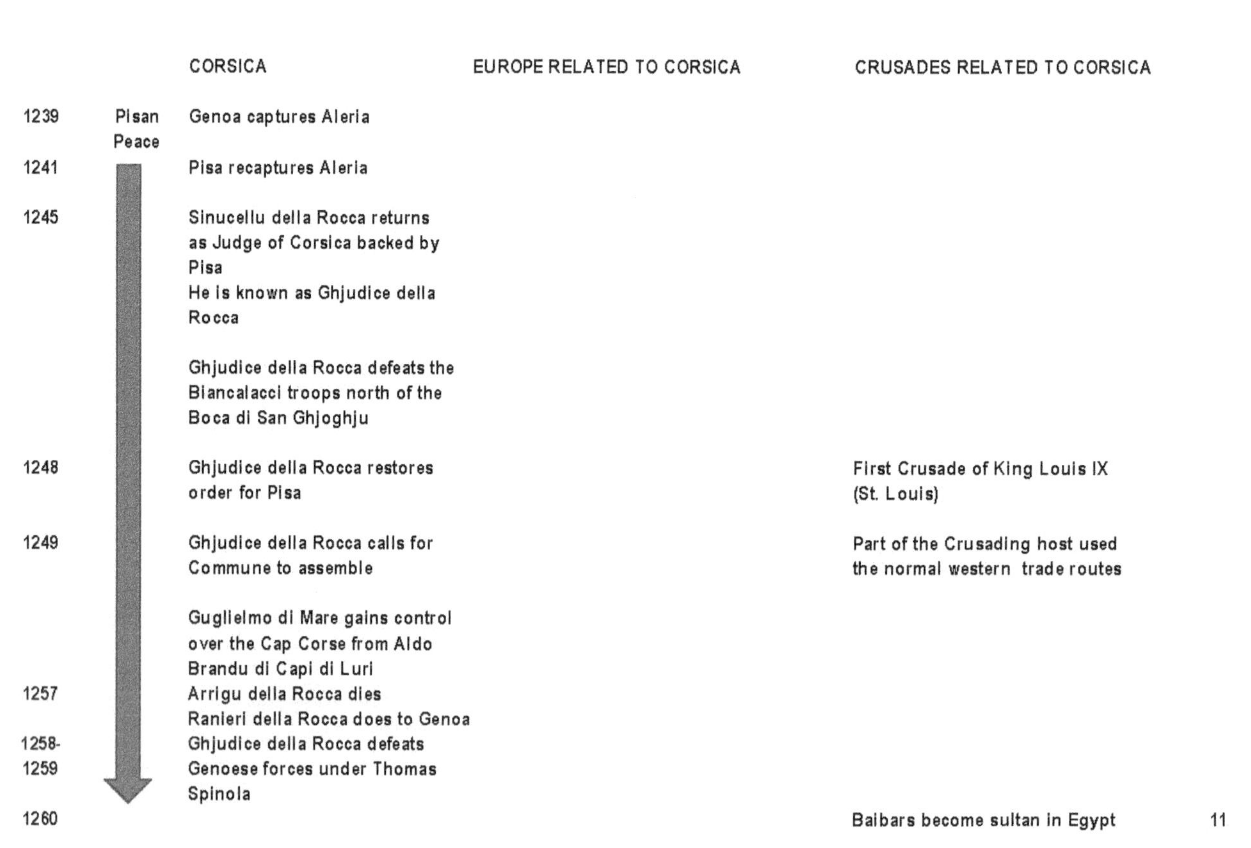

		CORSICA	EUROPE RELATED TO CORSICA	CRUSADES RELATED TO CORSICA
1239	Pisan Peace	Genoa captures Aleria		
1241		Pisa recaptures Aleria		
1245		Sinucellu della Rocca returns as Judge of Corsica backed by Pisa He is known as Ghjudice della Rocca Ghjudice della Rocca defeats the Biancalacci troops north of the Boca di San Ghjoghju		
1248		Ghjudice della Rocca restores order for Pisa		First Crusade of King Louis IX (St. Louis)
1249		Ghjudice della Rocca calls for Commune to assemble		Part of the Crusading host used the normal western trade routes
		Guglielmo di Mare gains control over the Cap Corse from Aldo Brandu di Capi di Luri		
1257		Arrigu della Rocca dies Ranieri della Rocca does to Genoa		
1258-1259		Ghjudice della Rocca defeats Genoese forces under Thomas Spinola		
1260				Baibars become sultan in Egypt

11

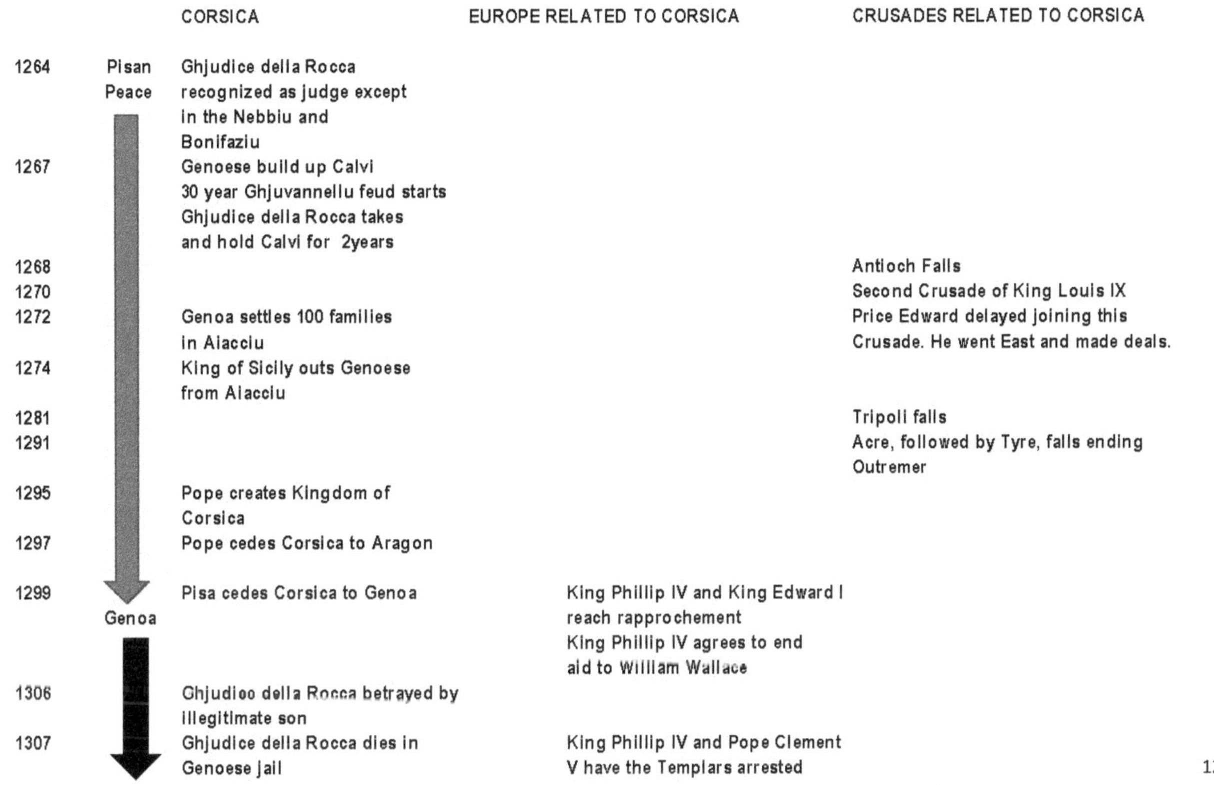
CORSICA
EUROPE RELATED TO CORSICA
CRUSADES RELATED TO CORSICA
1264	Pisan Peace	Ghjudice della Rocca recognized as judge except in the Nebbiu and Bonifaziu
1267	Genoese build up Calvi
30 year Ghjuvannellu feud starts
Ghjudice della Rocca takes and hold Calvi for 2years
1268	Antioch Falls
1270	Second Crusade of King Louis IX
1272	Genoa settles 100 families in Aiacciu	Price Edward delayed joining this Crusade. He went East and made deals.
1274	King of Sicily outs Genoese from Aiacciu
1281	Tripoli falls
1291	Acre, followed by Tyre, falls ending Outremer
1295	Pope creates Kingdom of Corsica
1297	Pope cedes Corsica to Aragon
1299	Pisa cedes Corsica to Genoa	King Phillip IV and King Edward I reach rapprochement
King Phillip IV agrees to end aid to William Wallace
Genoa
1306	Ghjudice della Rocca betrayed by illegitimate son
1307	Ghjudice della Rocca dies in Genoese jail	King Phillip IV and Pope Clement V have the Templars arrested
12